CHEERL[EADERS]

#35

MOVING UP

LESLIE DAVIS

SCHOLASTIC INC.
New York Toronto London Auckland Sydney

ISBN 0-590-41011-3

12 11 10 9 8 7 6 5 4 3 2 1   7 8 9/8 0 1 2/9

Printed in the U.S.A.   01

First Scholastic printing, November 1987

CHEERLEADERS

MOVING UP

CHEERLEADERS

CHAPTER 1

"**O**oooohhhhh."

One unanimous groan, the blending of the student voices in the bleachers, greeted the missed foul shot. Tarenton High's basketball team was losing so badly to Duxbury that kids were leaving the stands.

Olivia Evans, captain of the cheerleading squad, felt her heart sink. She pivoted from her spot in the front row and looked at the disgruntled faces behind her. Unfortunately she made eye contact with Diana Tucker, who mouthed, "Do something!" with her typical exaggerated concern. She's right, Olivia told herself, it's up to me. She couldn't do a thing about the way the boys were playing, but it was clearly her responsibility to do something about the lack of support they were getting from their schoolmates.

She chewed her lip as the team called a time-out. Think, Evans, think! " 'Up and at 'Em,' " she whispered harshly to Sean Dubrow, the seventeen-year-old next to her.

Sean, one of two male cheerleaders on the squad, turned his head as if he hadn't heard her correctly. " '*Up and at 'Em*'? We haven't rehearsed that in weeks! What gives?"

"We're losing by a mile — that's what gives," Olivia hurled back as she got to her feet. "Pass it on. Now!" she added as she hurried out onto the gym floor temporarily vacated by the team. It was a quick, peppy cheer requiring the fans to stand up and stamp their feet three times as two of the girls did scissor leaps. Maybe, Olivia thought, just maybe it would build the dwindling spirit and fire up the team. She tried to ignore the look of surprise on the faces of the four remaining squad members as they hurried out to join her. Peter Rayman arched his eyebrows at her and Tara Armstrong shook her head as she passed the word to Jessica Bennett and Hope Chang.

Questioning glances were all she got, however. Unity was everything in cheerleading, and each of them knew better than to question a call. Hope and Jessica got in formation between Olivia and Tara, hands at their waists, feet apart. Sean got behind Hope and when Jessica felt Peter's hands slide under hers, she knew he was in position. Jessica remembered to smile, remembered to make eye contact with the crowd, and hoped that she remembered the cheer. Even back on the bench, their coach, Ardith Engborg, looked as though she was trying to guess what Olivia's call had been.

As Peter braced himself behind Jessica, he

2

watched Hope get into position with Sean. They'd shared so much, especially those first uncertain days when they'd trained together at the cabin the previous August. He watched her scan the crowd, but his heart didn't ache anymore. Maybe he never really knew what he wanted. Straight, serious Hope with her chiseled features and her brilliant mind was bound to wind up with somebody from the honor society, somebody off to Harvard or Stanford after graduation, just like she planned to be. Somebody smart and talented, probably rich and great-looking, too. Somebody he'd never be able to compete with. Peter blinked. Olivia was raising her hand to begin the cheer.

Hope stood still, felt Sean's hands tighten around her waist, and raised her eyes to the bleachers. To the left, at the entrance to the gym, she caught sight of Patrick Henley, a graduate of last June and already successful in his moving and garbage hauling business. When he stepped aside, a figure in a sheepskin jacket, collar up against the wind, looked out at her and gave her a thumbs-up motion with his gloved hand. Tony Pell, Tarenton's "Tough Tony," then doubled over with imagined hunger pains and pointed to his wristwatch. "Pizzaaaaaa . . ." he mouthed. Hope grinned at him and then turned her attention to her captain, who had cupped her mouth with her hands and was calling to the students, " 'Up and at 'Em,' 'Up and at 'Em,' let's go!"

A jolt slammed Peter's heart against his ribs as he supported Jessica. Tony Pell! Of all the guys in the world, Tony was the very last one he'd ever pick for Hope. He'd been in trouble, was always

3

on the edge of some hassle or another. He didn't even go to Tarenton High, but to the district's vocational school. It wasn't the first time Peter had sighed and wondered what Hope was trying to prove by seeing the guy.

At either end of the line, Olivia and Tara cupped their ears. "Let me hear it!" they called.

"Show us your spirit!" the four in between them added.

The crowd in the stands rose and gave three quick stamps. "Go, Wolves! Go, Wolves! Go, Wolves!" the entire gym cried as Peter and Sean bent into the leap and supported the girls in front of them. Hope rose effortlessly into the air. But as Peter tried to lift Jessica, he grabbed only a fist full of her sweater. She was thrown just millimeters off balance as Peter shifted, frantically trying to keep her from falling. Her outstretched arm hit Olivia's shoulder, and Jessica started to tumble.

"I'm losing it," Jessica cried, as she felt Peter grab the wool of her sweater. Her arm sent Olivia back to the right as Jessica came down, not on her toes, but on the side of her right foot. It buckled under her and Jessica collapsed in a heap on the polished wooden floor. The students rose to watch.

Blushing into the roots of her brown hair, Jessica struggled up, shrugging off the offers of help. She tried desperately to focus on the injury rather than the hundreds of faces she knew were staring at her.

"I'm fine," she muttered to Peter and Sean as she put her weight on her left foot. Willing her-

4

self to walk, she gritted her teeth and took a step forward. The bleachers had never seemed so far away! Pain, hot and sharp, shot from her right ankle into the joint and up the back of her leg. She shut her eyes and fell onto one knee. Then Patrick was beside her.

"I've got her," Patrick Henley said as he turned, with Jessica held against him, to face Coach Engborg. His grip tightened as Jessica opened her green eyes and tears brimmed over her lashes. "Hurts, Jessica?"

She nodded, and as the rest of her squad made their way back to their seats, Patrick followed the coach and team doctor to the door to the girls' locker room.

"I'm sorry," Jessica continued to whisper as Patrick eased her onto the narrow bench between the lockers. Coach Engborg patted Jessica's arm and helped her unlace her sneaker.

The tug of Jessica's shoe, even the removal of her sock, sent needle sharp slivers of pain through her and she clung to Patrick's hand to keep from moaning. The physician poked the swelling and rotated Jessica's ankle. "Doesn't appear to be broken, but the bones on the foot can be very tricky. I'll call an ambulance and get you a nice, safe ride to Haven Lake Medical Center. Henry Chang's orthopedic department is the best around. They'll have you fixed up in no time. We'll have your parents meet you there."

"No!" flew from her throat and she knew they were all staring at her. "No," she repeated, attempting to sound more controlled. "Please don't put me in an ambulance. My parents went out to dinner and shopping. I can pack it in ice, I know what to do. I can't have an X ray without them, anyway." She began to feel panicky. "Please don't put me in an ambulance."

The coach touched her arm. "Jessica, I have the medical waiver your mother signed. It's for emergencies just like this. You know she'd want you to be looked at right away."

As she spoke, the doctor cracked a cold pack and wrapped the injury. "It needs immediate attention, young lady, if you want to resume your cheerleading career. Let me call the ambulance."

Patrick felt Jessica's grip crush the knuckles of his fingers. The color had drained from her complexion.

"I'll drive her. No problem. I've got my truck, nice wide seat and an extra strong seatbelt." He looked at the skeptical faces of the adults. "Come on, you know I own a hauling business. I move people's valuables every day. I know just how to handle precious cargo." He smiled down at Jessica's expression of relief. "I'll stay with you, Jessica, and see that you get home, safe and sound."

"I'm being an awful lot of trouble," Jessica replied weakly.

"No way," Patrick said. "Besides, after all my years in this school, this is the first chance I've had to see the inside of the girls' locker room." Her smile made him relax a little. He knew from his own bout with pneumonia and from the hospitalization of his former business partner Pres Tilford, of Jessica's dread of all medical institutions. He could only imagine what the thought of

6

riding in an ambulance was doing to her. The best medicine Patrick had to offer was his humor and his presence, and another look at the doctor and coach told him they agreed.

Ardith Engborg pulled the medical form from her clipboard. "Jessica's insurance company and policy number are right there, and here's her mother and stepfather's signatures. I'll square things with the rest of the squad and see you at the hospital as soon as I can get away. Be careful with her, Patrick."

He laughed. "Coach, you know I'll just pretend Jessica's somebody's priceless vase."

"That's better than pretending I'm somebody's bag of trash," Jessica added, making them all laugh. Clowning and teasing were natural parts of Patrick's personality, but so were maturity and responsibility. Jessica had seen glimpses of all sides of him since they'd been dating. Now gratitude flooded through her as he took charge, gathered her things, and carried her to his truck. She realized that the confidence the team doctor and Coach Engborg had in him were all that kept her from having been rushed to Haven Lake Medical Center in an ambulance with sirens screaming and lights flashing. As Patrick lowered her onto her good foot, she clapped her hands over her ears at the imagined sound.

"Jessica?"

She shook her head. "It's nothing. Just help me into the truck."

True to his word, Patrick drove slowly and carefully from the parking lot of the high school,

7

across town, and down the country road to the medical center. "This is where everybody goes for sports injuries, Jessica. Hope Chang's father is one of the best bone doctors around," he said, trying to make conversation.

Jessica nodded and closed her eyes. "I know, but he won't be there at this time of night."

Patrick took one hand from the wheel and patted her arm. "The rest of the department's just as good as he is." He stole a glance at her as the streetlights washed over them. She looked as though she were in pain, but he couldn't tell if the ankle was causing it or her fear of hospitals.

Jessica Bennett had come a long way since the death of her father when she was younger, from someone unwilling to risk caring about anybody again, to a young woman who knew eventually she'd be able to fall in love . . . some day. . . .

She felt Patrick looking at her and turned to catch his smile. "I'm glad you were there tonight," she whispered.

"I'm glad I was, too. We'll get this taken care of in no time. You'll see, Jessica. I know how much you hate hospitals." He was silent as the lights of the hospital came into view. As they got closer, he touched her arm again. "Before your father died, did he ever — did your mother have to call an ambulance, Jessica?"

In reply, she snapped on the radio and found a rock station, filling the silence with the twang of electric guitars. Patrick took the hint and dropped the subject, but as he drove up to the emergency entrance, his hands tightened on the wheel. Don't pull away from me, Jessica, he said to himself. Let me help.

From her seat on the bleachers, the scenario unfolded in front of Diana Tucker like a soap opera. She hadn't missed a thing, since she spent every game studying the moves of the cheerleading squad she intended to join, one way or another. Hope was grinning at somebody on the sidelines; Peter had been too busy watching Hope, and the look on Jessica's face told Diana that she couldn't remember the cheer. Diana's heart had jumped as Jessica fell, but not from concern. Since her first day at Tarenton High, the transplanted Californian had wanted nothing but to become a member of the squad. It was top priority with her, and she'd tried just about every trick in the book to get there.

How romantic, she thought, as Patrick Henley came out of nowhere to scoop Jessica into his arms and carry her into the locker room. What a golden opportunity for me! If Jessica only missed a game or two, it still gave Diana the chance to talk to Coach Engborg about finding a substitute. As the game resumed, the coach came out of the locker room and huddled on the bench with the squad. Her expression, her body language, everything about the situation told Diana what she needed to know. Jessica Bennett was out of commission. Diana could be a cheerleader before the end of the season!

Jessica's green eyes still brimmed with tears as she dabbed them with a tissue as she sat on the

9

table in the examining room of the emergency department. The light was harsh and artificially bright, and everything smelled of antiseptic and disinfectant. As much as her ankle ached, the commotion in her stomach was worse. Butterflies were dancing around as if they were trying to escape; her palms were sweaty and her pulse was racing. Over and over she watched the door for sight of Patrick as she told herself to calm down. After he'd given the medical form to the admitting desk, he'd stayed with her, right through the X ray in radiology, but now he was out in the lobby at the pay phones, calling her mother and stepfather.

"Hey, Jessica!" Patrick's voice broke through her concentration, and she smiled with relief.

"Thank goodness! Patrick, I thought you'd never come back," she cried. He came to sit next to her on the table and she leaned against him.

He put his arm around her shoulder. "There's still no answer at your house, but the coach has arrived. She's out in the hall, talking with the nurse at the desk."

Just the feel of Patrick's arm made Jessica's panic lessen. They were interrupted by the coach and by the doctor, who had Jessica's X ray in her hand.

"Young lady, I've got good news. There's no break. The pain should decrease steadily as the swelling goes down. Keep it cold tonight and stay off it. Ten days ought to do it. I suspect it's more of a bruise than anything else."

Coach Engborg held up a pair of crutches. "Compliments of our school physician," she said.

"Follow doctor's orders and we'll have you back on the gym floor in no time."

The doctor helped her from the table onto her good foot. "If there's no improvement in forty-eight hours, make an appointment with Dr. Chang." She glanced at Jessica's uniform. "I certainly hope Tarenton won the game tonight in your honor."

Jessica tried to smile back at the doctor. "Thanks, but there wasn't much hope of a victory." If they hadn't been losing so badly in the first place and Olivia hadn't been so desperate to build the team's spirit by using an unfamiliar cheer, none of it might have happened. She sighed but kept the thought to herself as the coach helped her with the crutches.

When the doctor had gone, Coach Engborg looked at her watch. "Your squad members send their love. I tried to talk them out of stopping by your house tonight, but I'm not sure I did a very good job. If they do show up, you're still to follow orders. Patrick, see that she keeps that foot elevated. I can't afford permanent injury in a star like Jessica."

Jessica smiled, grateful for the humor, but then she gave her coach a serious look. "I'm out for two weeks. It'll mess up almost all the routines. You'll have to start from scratch, extra practice and everything."

"Can't be helped," Ardith Engborg replied. She looked at Patrick. "Get her home safely. I'll call in the morning. Jessica, there's nothing to be done now. It wasn't your fault. These things

11

happen. I'm just sorry I don't have a backup." She waved good-bye to them and headed out for her car.

Out of sight of Patrick and Jessica, the coach shook her head. It *would* foul up everything, no doubt about that. It would mean more strain on the squad and modifying the cheers to fit an odd, rather than even, number of cheerleaders. She shivered into her coat and drew it around her as she crossed the parking lot. It was time to do what she should have done all along. As coach, she needed to come up with a fair, equitable plan to choose an alternate cheerleader. It might be too late for her to do anything about the gap Jessica would leave, but as coach it was her responsibility to see that the squad wasn't put in this position again.

Jessica leaned on her crutches. With the doctor and coach gone, she'd expected to feel relief, but she was still fighting sweaty palms and anxiety. She blinked hard and took her first steps, trying not to look at the cabinets full of medical supplies.

Patrick picked up her jacket, purse, and sneaker. "Wait here, I'll go warm up the truck and drive right up to the door."

"No," she whispered as harshly as she had in the locker room. "Let me go with you — please don't leave me here again by myself. I know I'm being silly. I know. Patrick, just get me out of here, please."

He hugged her, crutches and all. "Jessica," he

12

whispered back, "nobody's going to leave you this time." A surge of emotion made him warm all over. If only she needed him like this all the time, life would be perfect. He made his way slowly, watching the bright overhead lights reflect in her dark hair. Patrick hoped her parents would stay out for hours so he could be the one to help, to make her comfortable, to take care of her.

"We've nearly made it," he added as they left the medical center. "The truck's right over there."

As the door swung closed behind them, Jessica put her face up to the moonlight and inhaled deeply. "Oh, I feel better already. Patrick, I really appreciate this. I couldn't have made it without you tonight. I hope the squad does decide to stop at the house. I need to apologize to everybody, and I could sure use some cheering up."

Patrick smiled bravely and tried not to feel hurt. Someday, he knew, Jessica would see how great they'd be together — not just in an emergency, but forever.

CHAPTER

2

By the time Patrick had driven Jessica back to her house, the group had gathered and was waiting for her. "It looks as though I'm giving a party," she exclaimed as they rounded the corner. Her parents' car sat in the driveway and other cars lined the curb.

"Diana Tucker's!" Jessica pointed to a white Volkswagen behind Sean's Fiero. "What is she doing here?"

"Probably just wants to gloat," Patrick replied, only half kidding.

Jessica nodded glumly. "You're right. This is her golden opportunity to point out what a klutz I am."

Patrick parked and came around to help her out. "You can be klutzy any time, if it means I get to play hero."

"Oh, Patrick," she said.

He grinned at her. "Oh, Jessica."

When they got to the front door, Abby Bennett pulled her daughter into a hug, crutches and all. "The phone was ringing when we got home," she said breathlessly. "It was your coach, but she said Patrick had taken care of everything and you were on your way home. Thank goodness for Patrick," she added, giving him a smile. "If your ankle isn't bothering you too much, your friends can stay a little while . . . school night, you know, Jessica. But you should sit on the couch and keep that ankle elevated."

Jessica kissed her mother's cheek. "I'm fine, really, now that I'm home, anyway. The worst part is no cheerleading for ten days."

Abby Bennett looked sympathetic as Patrick and her daughter headed for the family room. When they got to the doorway, Patrick said, "Tah dah!" and a cheer rose from the crowd, which was a blur of red and white uniforms to Jessica.

"What, no cast we can autograph?" somebody called.

"Did they X ray it?"

"How long will you be on the bench?"

"Hey, guys, let Jessica catch her breath! Come on, she needs the couch to elevate the injury."

Jessica blinked and looked at the person making the final comments and hushing everybody else. Diana Tucker, in her California-girl outfit of stirrup pants and a huge cable-knit sweater, was busy shooing Olivia and Tara from their seats and fluffing the pillows. Diana? Jessica had prepared herself for the junior's usual sarcasm, and suddenly she was all sympathy and concern.

15

"Here you go," Diana continued, showing Jessica the space she'd made. "We'll only stay as long as you want us. Then you can get some rest."

"Thanks, Diana," Jessica replied.

"Can I get you some aspirin or a soda?"

Jessica looked at Patrick and back. "No, thanks, they gave me some aspirin in the emergency room. I'm fine, now."

Tara Armstrong wrinkled her nose at Diana and patted Jessica's shoulder. Even after all the cheerleading, Tara's beautiful red hair was still perfect, her uniform still fresh. "Your fall was the highlight of the evening, I'm afraid."

"We lost?"

Tara looked quickly at Olivia and then back. "Yes. Even with Olivia's last-ditch effort to fire up the team, we lost."

On the other side of Diana, Olivia felt her face redden. It had been her fault, the whole miserable thing. No matter what her reasons for doing it, she'd insisted on an unfamiliar cheer and now a squad member was injured. She wanted to crawl under the couch. Sometimes she hated the responsibility of being captain. When things went well, it was great to get the credit, but when something like this happened, it was awful. Totally awful. Olivia sighed and put Jessica's crutches against the wall. She wanted to apologize, but there were too many people in the room.

Behind the girls, against the wall, Sean Dubrow was looking through the Bennett tape collection while Peter Rayman turned on the stereo. Peter fooled with the dials so he wouldn't have to stare at Hope and Tony. He sighed. As if having to be

16

in the same room with the two of them weren't enough, he could hear them asking Jessica about her injury. He groaned to himself as he imagined Jessica telling the truth. "It was all Peter's fault. He was staring at you, Hope, and not paying attention. . . ." Clod, he thought to himself. He wasn't the natural show-off that Sean was; he was a gymnast, all right, but didn't this stupid accident prove that he had no business out on a gym floor in front of hundreds of fans? Not long ago Hope had talked him into entering the Young Mr. Tarenton contest and he'd had the good sense to quit, right in the middle, when he realized it wasn't his thing.

Sean handed Peter a cassette and he put it in the tape deck. Maybe cheerleading wasn't his thing, either. Peter wished there was a hole in the floor he could sink into.

"Tough break, isn't it?"

He stood up at the sound of a girl's voice. It was Diana, and she was smiling sympathetically. "About Jessica, I mean," she continued. "But, you know, Peter, it's bad times like this when a squad can really show its stuff. You guys are the best around and you can pull together and prove to Jessica that you can carry on till she gets back."

Sympathy? From Diana? "I guess we'll have to," he mumbled. "I'm just glad it wasn't anything more serious."

She patted his arm and Sean's, too. "I know just how you must feel, having your attention broken at the critical moment. Once on my old squad in Santa Barbara, I was just about to do a handspring when I caught sight of my boyfriend

17

with the class flirt. I landed flat on my back — can you believe it?"

What Peter couldn't believe was her attitude. While it was just like jealous Diana to point out the fact that she'd seen him staring at Hope, it was definitely out of character for her to admit that she'd made a mistake — an embarrassing one! Forgetting that he had never before heard Diana claim to have actually been a cheerleader at her old school, he stared up at her.

"*You* fell in front of everybody?"

"Only once, but once was enough."

"Now that must have been something to see," Sean added.

"It was, believe me," Diana answered and then made her way across the room. Sean looked at Peter. Peter looked at Sean. Together they lifted their shoulders in a silent question. *What gives with her?*

Abby Bennett let everyone stay until the tape was finished, and then broke up the visit. As the group left, Patrick stayed in the family room to grab a few minutes alone with Jessica. He kissed her tenderly while her parents were at the front door.

"I'll drive you to school and then swing by and drive you home," he said as he got into his jacket.

Jessica smiled up at him. "I'll take the drive to school, but you have a business to run. Don't change your schedule just because I'm on crutches."

"That's one of the great things about being in business for myself. I'm the boss."

She laughed. "I'd say the people waiting for

18

their furniture to arrive might have something to say about that!"

"Trust me, Jessica. I can make *everybody* happy."

Diana Tucker hadn't had a date for the game, and now as she drove herself home, it gave her time to think. She wasn't even playing the car stereo as she drove through the dark streets toward her house in Tarenton's fashionable neighborhood. Ten days on the bench . . . half the squad thinking Jessica's fall had been their fault . . . guilt and carelessness. What she could do with those emotions.

She smiled to herself as she thought about the look Sean and Peter had given each other. "You're about to see a brand-new Diana Tucker," she said out loud. From the moment Patrick Henley had carried Jessica off the floor, she'd been thinking about the situation, thinking about the squad and the coach, and mostly thinking that the golden opportunity had finally presented itself.

The only thing left to figure out was the best way to make all of it work in her favor. From her spot in the bleachers, one thing had been clear: The accident was the result of a combination of things, not just the fault of one person. But from what she could tell from her night at the Bennetts', at least three of the cheerleaders thought they were the only ones to blame.

She swung the Volkswagen carefully into her driveway and let the engine idle while she thought it through. Trying to come between the squad members hadn't worked. As much as they fought among themselves, she'd already learned that they'd join forces against an outsider. Diana winced, remembering her previous disastrous attempts at breaking up the squard. No, the way to get a place on the squad was through their hearts and the heart of their coach. She'd see to it that Coach Engborg considered the idea of a substitute cheerleader, and she'd see to it that the position was filled by one very able newcomer from California.

"I think maybe we ought to eat on paper plates until you come out of your fog, Mary Ellen," Pres Tilford said to his new wife, as they did their dinner dishes together.

Mary Ellen blinked and caught the plate that had nearly slipped through her soapy fingers. She and Pres, both cheerleaders before their graduation from Tarenton High, had married young, and with every passing day, it seemed more and more to Mary Ellen that it was the smartest thing she'd ever done. Sometimes she felt that Pres knew her better than she knew herself, especially when something was troubling her.

He was right, too, she was in a fog. Quickly, she rinsed the plate and handed it to him, watching as he dried it and added it to the stack of their new china in the cabinet. Pres was used to the best of everything, but it was Mary Ellen whose heart would have broken if she'd chipped the beautiful porcelain wedding gifts that, to protect, they washed by hand rather than in the dishwasher. "I'm sorry," she murmured. "There's just so much to think about."

"Because Garrison High wants you as their cheerleading coach, and that makes you feel like a traitor. Maybe it should, Melon."

She winced at her nickname. "If only the school weren't our arch rival. If only it were some brand-new school, or one not in the conference. Oh, Pres, it's more than Garrison. Just look at you. You and Patrick had a business, your very own business. You found something you were good at, something you enjoyed. Now, at Tartenton Fabricators, you love going to work, you love figuring out ways to expand, you love the challenge. Pres, that's what I want to feel."

"I guess I never thought of it like that," he answered softly.

Mary Ellen pulled the stopper and watched the water drain. "Look at me. I tried to make it in New York; I tried modeling. It didn't work. I came back to Tarenton, feeling like a failure. I tried day care. I'm not going to give up on college, but. . . . What am I really good at, Pres? What can I do better than just about anybody else? Cheerleading, that's what. I'm great at the gymnastic moves, at the timing, the balance. Teaching it should be the perfect answer. If only — "

"It wasn't at Garrison High School," Pres finished for her.

She nodded. "It couldn't be more wrong. I know what everybody will think. I know people will feel as though I'm a traitor, but it's a chance to do something I love."

She turned and faced Pres, her eyes shining. "Until there's a better place, I don't see what other choice I have. And at least for now, I'm going to do it. But I need your support. I'm sure not going to get any from anybody else."

Pres looked doubtful. "I want to support you, Mary Ellen, but it's not easy."

"Neither is being married, sometimes, but look at how great it is for us."

Pres pulled her into a hug. "You're right about that," he whispered, hoping she was as right about the coaching job.

They were interrupted by a knock at the door, and Pres and Mary Ellen looked at each other. They had a carriage house, formerly part of an estate in the Fable Point section of Tarenton, and a knock on the door way out there was unexpected.

Mary Ellen looked out the darkened window. "I think it's Patrick's truck!"

Pres opened the door as his former business partner stepped over the threshold. "Hey, what's up? You're a long way from home!"

"Down, actually. What's down is Jessica. She fell tonight at the game and bruised the bones in her foot." He settled onto the couch to tell them the whole story, and to add that his work schedule might have to be modified to help Jessica get around. Pres readily agreed to give him a hand with the moving business if it was needed.

After he'd gone, Mary Ellen looked at Pres. "Even Garrison has a permanent substitute who suits up and sits with the squad."

"Don't start comparing one against the other," Pres warned. "At least not to anybody but me."

She nodded. "You're right, but Coach Engborg should give it some serious thought."

Pres smiled. "I think we better let Coach Engborg take care of Tarenton's squad and let Coach Tilford take care of Garrison's."

"Sometimes you give great advice, Pres."

His smile widened into a grin. "I advised you to marry me, didn't I?"

By second period of the next day, Jessica had gotten the hang of maneuvering through the halls on her crutches. The swelling in her ankle had gone down almost overnight, leaving only a sharp pain if she put any weight on her foot.

Patrick had dropped her off with a kiss and a promise to be back at the last bell, but she still insisted that she wanted to sit in on cheerleading practice, at least the first day. She intended to hitch a ride home with Sean or one of the others with a car. One friend or another had carried her books to class, and though Diana Tucker hardly fit in the category of *friend*, she'd insisted on helping as they made their way to world history.

It was a class made up of juniors and seniors, one of the only two that both of them shared. Jessica gave Diana a grudging thank you as Diana put Jessica's books on her desk and made her way to her own seat. "I'm happy to help," Diana said, overly sweetly. "I can just imagine how awful you feel about the whole thing."

I bet you can, Jessica thought as she took her place and rummaged through her purse for a pencil. The class was in the midst of oral reports on Europe between the world wars. Jessica had already given her report on the Treaty of Versailles. It had been full of facts and as dry and boring as everybody else's. Nevertheless, good notes had to be taken as they were all to be tested when the last one was given.

The class was restless, the teacher making "shhhhh" noises, as Melissa Brezneski walked to the front of the room. She was a tall junior with classic features, although her long hair was always pulled back severely and she didn't dress with much style. Jessica didn't know her well but she often thought that if Melissa would just wear some makeup and funky clothes she'd improve about a thousand percent. In a lot of ways Melissa reminded Jessica of Hope. Melissa had the same dramatic face and dark hair as Hope, as well as being a brain, too.

Jessica cleared her thoughts and got ready to take notes. Melissa coughed, and looked around at her classmates, her brown eyes wide and serious. "We've been paying a lot of attention to dates and battles, but I'd like to talk about how that unrest affected a family. My grandmother was the prima ballerina with the Warsaw Ballet from 1935 until 1937, but she gave up everything to flee to America for freedom before Poland was again invaded in 1939."

The restlessness stopped; even the boys were paying attention as Melissa described her grandparents' flight through the mountains of Austria and Switzerland and the long, uncertain boat trip from Southhampton, England, to New York. "She was now a refugee, traveling through the same cities where she had danced and stayed at the finest hotels. She spoke perfect Polish and perfect French, but not a word of English. Because she

24

couldn't speak the language, people here thought she was uneducated and so she had to start all over again, and she did that through a language everyone understands." Melissa's voice grew hushed and she smiled. "She communicated through music and dance."

She held the class spellbound, telling real stories of the hardships, the fears, and the frustrations of life in those days. By the time she finished, Jessica was imagining, along with everyone else, the cold nights and uncertain days in which Madame Brezneski had lived. The invasion of Poland in 1939 wasn't just a date to be memorized, it was the end of a way of life and the beginning of another. She forgot all about her crutches and her ankle.

The class was still silent as Melissa finished and took her seat, and then spontaneous applause broke out. One of the boys even slapped her on the back in congratulations. Melissa smiled shyly.

Jessica shook her head and felt sorry for anybody who still had a report to give. There wasn't much that would live up to Melissa's. Later in the day as Jessica made her slow, clumsy way to the cafeteria, she was still thinking about the ballerina and her beloved city of Warsaw, Poland. As depressing as it was not to be able to cheer for two weeks, at least she'd be back on the squad. She couldn't imagine how awful it would be to know that not only would she never cheer again in Tarenton, but that, without warning, she'd be forced to leave for a new country, saying good-bye to her home forever.

CHAPTER

It took her so long to get to the cafeteria that she missed half the lunch period and by the last bell at the end of the day, Jessica was tired, *starving*, and her whole body ached from the crutches. She knew the best thing to do would be to take Patrick up on his offer and go home where she could rest. She also knew, however, that she owed something to the squad. Somehow, showing up for practice felt like an apology for all the extra practice they'd need because of her.

Peter Rayman stood at his locker exchanging the books from his last class for the ones he'd need for homework. The hall was alive with the clanging of lockers and the jubilant voices of rushing students as they called to one another. Some pulled on coats and rushed to waiting buses; others were off to the parking lot or clubs and sports practice. Peter was oblivious to all of it.

His stomach was in knots, as he slammed his locker and gave the combination lock a twist.

It's only practice, he kept telling himself, pressing his hand against the knot in his stomach. But it was practice without Jessica. He should have apologized to her quietly when he'd had the chance at her house. He should have said something to Coach Engborg when he'd passed her in the hall. Now he had to face everybody, including Hope. He hated thinking about it.

"How about fifty cents, then?"

Peter turned and nearly bumped into Tara Armstrong. She threw her head back and laughed in that confident way she had, letting her red hair fly.

"What?" he managed to say.

"I just offered you a penny for your thoughts, but you're in such a daze you didn't even hear me, so now I'm offering fifty cents. They must be important to have you so spaced."

Peter slung his backpack over his shoulder and started down the hall. "Not exactly."

Tara continued to walk next to him, acknowledging half a dozen other seniors as they called to her. "Well, since we're heading for the same place, I figure I've got from here to the locker rooms to worm it out of you."

Peter wanted to say, don't bother. Gorgeous, sometimes self-centered, Tara had enough confidence for both of them. The last thing he needed was her teasing.

"Shall I guess?"

"I wish you'd cut it out, Tara."

"Okay, okay but in about ten minutes you're going to have to be all pep and energy while we learn a bunch of new cheers. I just thought I could get you in the right mood." She hesitated as they pushed through the double doors and continued past the library. "That's it, isn't it, Peter? You're feeling guilty as all get out over Jessica."

He was quiet.

"Well?"

Peter stopped and stared at her. "I ought to feel guilty. Wouldn't you? If I hadn't been so hung up about Hope and Tony. . . ." He gritted his teeth, angrier than ever. He'd said too much and he could feel the color seeping up his neck.

Tara looked at him, but her expression was full of sympathy. "I had no idea you still cared about her."

"I don't. Not that way, but as a friend. And I just think she's making a crazy mistake hanging around with Tony. They don't have one thing in common." They started walking again and up ahead Peter could see Sean push open the door to the locker room.

"Maybe Hope needs to let loose, and Tony's her chance. There's more to life than violins and the honor society. He might be a way for her to find that out. If he cares about her, who's to get hurt?"

"She might."

"Well, that's a chance Hope seems willing to take. Maybe Tony sees another side of life in Hope, too. You know, more than fast cars and punk hair. Maybe she's good for Tony."

Peter groaned. "I'll never understand girls. The whole situation's pathetic."

Tara put her hand on the door marked GIRLS' LOCKER ROOM. "You can't do much about it, so why get all uptight? See you in a minute," she added, and before he could reply, she disappeared behind the door.

The practice session began with everyone gathered in the wrestling room. "I want the mats under you," Coach Engborg told them as she described her ideas for modifying the cheers. Jessica sat down against the wall and watched as her squad went through their warm-ups. Even she could tell that they were no more pulled together than the individual warm-up suits and sweat shirts they were wearing. Sean, his usual boisterous self, was doing handsprings while Peter hardly managed to run in place. Hope seemed deep in thought as she bent into deep-knee exercises. Olivia bumped into Tara and glared at her. The shrill sound of the coach's whistle made them all stop.

"All of you," their coach said, "sit right there on the mat."

Once they were seated next to each other, Ardith Engborg looked from one to the other. "I've got some great ideas, some modifications of what we're already doing, and some brand-new cheers, all of them designed for an odd number. It's good stuff and it will carry us through the next two weeks — *unless* you continue to act the way you were a minute ago."

From where Jessica was sitting she could see

the embarrassment on their faces. Olivia blushed and Peter squirmed. "I hate to lecture, but you deserve it," the coach continued. "Listen to this little pep talk so I don't have to repeat myself. You're a team, you're a unit, the best in the region. But what makes any cheering squad great is its unified spirit. I don't care if you've got boy or girl friend trouble, whether you've just flunked a test, or even if you think you're responsible for the injury of a fellow cheerleader." She waited. Five pairs of eyes looked at the mat. "You have to put those feelings aside when you're on the floor. You have to move, think, and cheer together. Olivia's your captain. She called for 'Up and At 'Em' to build up the fans' spirit. She used her best judgment for the situation. The rest of the mess happened from a combination of things: poor timing, lack of attention, self-doubt. You might say Jessica's fall was a group effort." She sighed, glad to see some faint smiles appearing. "She's not badly hurt, the squad will survive, and we'll be better than ever — *if we all pull together.*"

Right down the line, everybody began to relax. "One more thing," Coach Engborg added. "I use *we* because I'm feeling guilty, too. All season I've put off doing anything about adding a permanent substitute to the squad and now when we need one, it's too late. That's because of my poor judgment, and now you'll have to work twice as hard to compensate. Okay? We're all guilty and we're all forgiven. Now let's get to work!"

They got to their feet and gathered around the

coach, their energy back. By the end of the day's session, the group was as determined to make the new cheers as outstanding as they were back in the summer when they'd practiced together for the first time. When Coach Engborg blew her whistle again, it was to signal the end of the practice, and she was relieved to see five happily exhausted faces turn to her one last time.

"Announcement," she called before they headed for the locker rooms. "The Tarenton High Varsity-Alumni game is two weeks away. Jessica will be back with us, so we can use our regular routines. The PTA is using this as a fundraiser for sports equipment, so they want to raise as much money as possible. *We'll* be cheering for the alumni players, and the old cheerleaders will be cheering for Varsity. I've been told they want all the cheerleaders from past years, to make it as corny as possible. They're going through yearbooks to copy old uniforms, anything from knee-length box-pleated skirts and knee socks to red and white bloomers. If any of your parents went to Tarenton, ask them how much they remember and tell them to come! You might be able to come up with some old letter sweaters and jackets."

"Hey, that would make us traitors — we're for Varsity!" Sean said.

Their coach laughed. "It's all in good fun, and the wilder the night, the more money will be raised. I'm going to ask Mary Ellen Tilford to coach the alumni cheerleaders, though I hardly think of her as being old enough to have been graduated."

"Speaking of traitors . . ." Tara added.

"That's hardly fair," Coach Engborg replied.

"Hardly fair! She's coaching the Garrison squad. She's probably teaching them everything we've spent years perfecting."

"That's her job, Tara."

Sean shrugged his shoulders and broke in. "Pres is rich. She doesn't even need to work."

"Chauvinist!" cried Tara, momentarily forgetting her gripe with Mary Ellen.

Their coach sighed, wanting to tell them that there was more to working than money, but she'd lectured them enough for one day. Instead she said, "Mary Ellen deserves a chance," and shooed them into the locker rooms.

While her squad changed and headed for home, Ardith Engborg sat in her office, deep in thought. They needed a substitute, even though it was too late to help with the current problem. Next it would be up to the coach to figure out how she would incorporate a new member into the existing group. She sighed again. It was going to take diplomacy, energy, and time. Every year at tryouts it seemed half the student body wanted a place as cheerleader, and every year she felt she'd broken hundreds of hearts when the cuts were made. She had problems more serious than boy or girl friend trouble, flunked tests, or guilt. She'd have to devise a way to come up with one new member from the hundreds who would want a chance. If only she could just pick up the phone and have Mary Ellen back till the end of the season. She laughed at herself as she got up and turned off the light. Poor Mary Ellen had her own problems to deal with.

Out in the parking lot, Hope slid Jessica's books into the back of Sean's Fiero and he put the crutches on the floor. When Jessica had lowered herself into the passenger seat, Sean leaned over her from the steering wheel and looked at Hope. "We can squeeze you in here, too. Patrick might want Jessica to have a chaperon, anyway. You know how I drive girls wild."

Both girls made a face at him, and Hope shook her head. "Thanks, I've got a ride. He'll be here any minute." She watched as Sean and Jessica left, and didn't miss the look they gave each other. She was getting used to the disapproval, or at least the lack of understanding, from her friends. Even she had to admit that Tony Pell was the furthest thing from anyone else she'd ever been interested in. Maybe that's why he was exciting. Sometimes she didn't know, herself.

Tony arrived as Sean disappeared around the corner, and leaned over to open the door of his family's car for her. "Big, bad day with the books?"

Hope shook her head. "Big, bad day with the coach. She let us have it from every angle. It worked, though." They made conversation over the rock music blaring from his stereo cassette, and she finally turned it off when they reached the low, modern Chang house.

"Hope, you're probably the only kid in Tarenton that doesn't like New Wave."

"*Who* doesn't," she automatically corrected his grammar. "At this time of day it gives me a headache." This time and any time, she added silently. She was under enough pressure from home to excel at the classics on her violin without having to pretend she liked what sounded like a string instrument in extreme pain. As the car engine idled, Hope touched Tony's arm. "Forget it. Come on in and have a Coke or something to eat. I'm starved."

"Think it's okay?"

"Sure," she replied, getting out of the car and leading him into the kitchen entrance. "I'm home," Hope called as they took off their jackets and she opened the refrigerator.

Caroline Chang's voice drifted from her studio and in a moment she appeared in the doorway. Hope's mother, an accomplished watercolor artist, looked startled to see Tony. She had her portfolio under her arm. "Hello, you two," she said.

"Hi," Tony replied.

Hope looked at her mother's doubtful expression. "We're going to play some tapes or something."

"Well . . . I was just about to take some of my work to the framer's. As long as Tony's here with his car, would you two mind picking up James at his karate lesson? I won't be able to get there in time, and I hate to rush when I'm picking out matting for my work."

Hope sighed. She could tell her mother didn't want them in the house alone.

"Sure thing, Mrs. Chang," Tony replied. "Hope can show me the way." He looked as though he had more interesting things on his mind than picking up a kid brother, but arguing was unthinkable in the Chang household. He and Hope stayed in the kitchen long enough to finish their sodas, and then drove to downtown Tarenton.

At the north end of Main Street, an old-fashioned brick building took up the end of the block. Street lights came on as Hope pointed to an empty parking space at the curb. BODYWORKS was emblazoned on the plate glass windows in gold leaf and under it in smaller letters, Tony read out loud, "Martial arts, jazz, ballet, and aerobic exercise. Phew, that's some combination!"

Hope elbowed him playfully as they entered the building. "I don't think you take them all at once." The first room on the right was a large, mat-filled area. Tony arched his eyebrows at the rows of women running in place.

"Looks like fun," Hope said, looking over his shoulder.

"Looks like work," he answered as they climbed the stairs. On the second floor, music drifted from behind practice room doors. While they waited for her brother James' class to finish, they peeked into another glass-paned door. A single figure floated through a series of graceful ballet moves. She was wrapped in leg warmers to her knees and wore a black leotard. Her dark hair was pulled back tight into a knot at the nape of her neck. Hope recognized her classmate.

"Melissa Brezneski," she whispered to Tony. "She's here almost every time we come for James. *Sleeping Beauty*," she added.

"She looks wide awake."

"The music, silly. She's dancing to Tchai-kovsky's *Sleeping Beauty*. He set the fairy tale to music a hundred years ago. I play it on the violin."

Tony watched briefly and then turned for the karate class. "If Sleeping Beauty's looking for Prince Charming, she ought to do something about her hair and where she spends her free time."

Hope let it pass, saying only "There's more to life than boyfriends, Tony." She turned back to watch. The dancer moved to the ballet strains in perfect synchronization, totally absorbed in her dance. As if she were focusing on an inner guide, she spun and then leaped over the hardwood floor, ignoring her reflection in the wall-sized mirror.

Unconsciously, Hope moved her head to the familiar music. She and Melissa shared some classes at school, and like Hope, Melissa had an interest outside of school which kept her from participating in most of the clubs and sports teams. The Changs had encouraged Hope to be a cheerleader to broaden her interests, and some-times Hope wondered if she belonged on the squad at all. Classical music was what she loved, playing it the way Melissa loved to move to it.

At the sound of the bell, Hope reluctantly turned away to join Tony at the door of her younger brother's karate class.

CHAPTER

4

Diana Tucker tapped her foot and looked at her Rolex for the tenth time. Back in Santa Barbara, for a teenager to own such an expensive, adult status symbol watch was the ultimate. Diana had pleaded, cried, thrown tantrums, and begged. Her parents had finally relented and bought her one to soften the blow that she had to move from sunny southern California to Tarenton.

What a joke! Tarenton! To Diana's way of thinking, it fell just short of the frozen tundra. Winter went on forever and to make matters worse, nobody knew or cared whether she had a Rolex or a toy watch from a McDonald's Happy Meal on her wrist. When somebody complimented her on her clothes, it was because they thought she'd shopped at Marnie's or some other boutique in the mall. How could they be so dumb?

With a sigh she got back to the problem at hand. Coach Engborg had disappeared into the principal's office while Diana had been in the guidance office, returning college catalogues. Diana had pretended to be busy while she waited for the coach to come out. However, there were less than two minutes until the bell for her algebra class, and the door marked PRINCIPAL was still closed.

Diana's heart thumped as the door opened. She scooped up the new catalogues she'd checked out, gave the coach time to begin down the corridor, and then caught up with her. "Coach Engborg, what a coincidence! I've been meaning to talk to you."

"I just have a minute, the bell's about to ring," the coach replied as she continued down the hall.

Diana matched her stride. "Me, too. I've got to run and meet Jessica and carry her books to algebra. What a shame about her fall. I'm glad I can help her get around, though. We share a few classes. She probably wouldn't be feeling nearly as guilty if the cheerleading squad had a substitute to fill in for her. Back on my old squad we had one. Every team in the league did."

"Yes, I'm sure it's a good idea," Ardith Engborg replied.

"Of course, this late in the season it would be tough to come up with a fair way to choose one. *If* you decided to, that is. Tryouts would just be hundreds of kids all over again, just for one little place. It would take forever! No, you'd probably be better off just appointing somebody, somebody who'd never tried out before, so there'd be no hard feelings."

As Diana finished, the bell rang and the quiet halls filled with the boisterous rush of classes changing. "But someone who knew the cheers and could jump right in and add to the spirit," the coach added.

"Yes, that's it," Diana said, making sure her blonde hair bounced and her expression was enthusiastic. "An underclass student, too, so she could move on with the squad next year."

"My thought, precisely. She — or he — could become a regular member."

"He?" Diana said.

Coach Engborg smiled. "We do have boys on the squad, too. Thanks for your thoughts. I'm off to the gym."

"Anytime," Diana replied, but she was already being jostled by the crowds hurrying around her. Boys! That thought had never occurred to her. Still, anyone who knew the cheers and "could jump right in" as Coach had said, would have tried out last spring, before Diana had transferred to Tarenton. If the coach made a rule that it had to be someone new, that virtually wiped out any competition. Diana Tucker, she told herself, you're in a class by yourself. She hurried off to meet Jessica, wishing she could do a handspring right there and clinch the appointment on the spot.

Mary Ellen Kirkwood Tilford grabbed her yogurt and salad and took a seat by herself in the teachers' lunchroom, off the main cafeteria of Garrison High School. Mary Ellen smiled to herself. At least once or twice a day a faculty member or student would stare as if trying to place her. Captain of the Tarenton High cheerleaders, just last year, she'd tell them. It always jogged their memory, and the reaction wasn't always pleasant. There were days when she thought she should wear a sign across her back, reading: I AM NOT A SPY FOR TARENTON.

Nobody was hostile at the moment, however, and she ate her yogurt alone so she could review the notes she'd been taking. She'd spent hours compiling lists of the cheers she'd done, what they'd entailed, and the years they'd been used.

While she ate she wrote "Up and At 'Em." That had been one of Pres and Angie Poletti's favorites, Olivia's too, when they'd all been on last year's squad together. She shook her head, knowing it was the one that had tripped up Jessica. *Hardly used*, she wrote next to it, thinking, perhaps, a variation might fit for Garrison.

The night before she'd worked hard at convincing Pres that this was what she wanted, this was where she belonged. Now she had to prove it, even to herself. For the moment, she intended to concentrate on what the Garrison cheerleaders already knew. It would be safest and most productive to polish their existing skills and synchronization. *Nothing new for now*, she jotted in the margin. Mary Ellen Tilford was not trying to change them. They were already good the way they were.

"Hope?"

Hope Chang turned from her locker. Diana Tucker was standing behind her. Diana fished through her purse, and as Hope waited, pulled out a cassette.

40

"This is a tape of some violin stuff," Diana said. "One of my father's patients gave it to him for Christmas, but he already has it. I thought you might like it, since it's classical — your taste in music."

Hope blinked and tried to decide whether Diana was being sarcastic. Diana could be the queen of sarcasm. "This is Perlman! He's one of the best in the world!"

Diana smiled. "Good, then you'll enjoy it. My father will be pleased that Dr. Chang's daughter has it." She glanced at her watch. "Time for class. See you later."

Hope looked once more at the tape in her hand and then back at the departing figure of Diana Tucker, disappearing through the crowd.

Jessica finished the day with a sigh. Her ankle ached; her leg ached from holding it just off the floor; her arms ached; her palms, wrists, and armpits were killing her; and she suspected there'd be a pop quiz in algebra in the morning. Life could be totally gross. Going to practice had been a dumb idea. She couldn't add a thing; she felt as though she was making everybody self-conscious, and it was Coach Engborg who finally suggested that she take the rest of the week to rest her foot. "You're an athlete, Jessica," she'd said. "You know you need rest. We want you back as soon as possible."

Jessica made her way home by bus without much trouble. She knew, as inviting as her house looked with its colonial blue shutters and fresh paint, it would be empty. Her mother worked at

Marnie's in the mall, and her stepfather, Daniel, spent every waking hour with his computers. Jessica fought the lump in her throat. From Patrick on down, they all had obligations and responsibilities much more important than playing host or nurse to an ailing cheerleader. They had real life to contend with.

Jessica let herself in and dropped her coat and books on the kitchen table. She thought about her mother and Daniel, busy in their own lives. She thought about Patrick and the successful business he'd built from scratch. What was *she* going to do with her own life, beyond trying not to flunk tomorrow's algebra quiz?

Diana Tucker revved the motor of her Volkswagen and waited impatiently for the long, yellow line of school buses to snake their way out onto the street. She watched as Melissa Brezneski walked across her line of vision and got into her own car. Diana's full blonde hair had two French braids at the temples, plaited with lavender ribbon to match her pleated pants. Even the thick flannel lining of her denim coat had lavender in it. Diana watched her classmate pass. Melissa's hair, as usual, was in a tight bun and her coat was a plain navy blue parka. A total mouse, Diana thought, without any sense of style.

Diana drummed her foot and watched the last bus pass, catching sight of Jessica sitting behind the driver. Jessica on the bus! Why hadn't she thought about how the cheerleader would get home? It would have been the perfect opportunity to get in one more good deed before the end of the day. One more way to pretend she was interested in the injury and sympathetic to her situation. It had never been more important to make friends with as many of the squad as possible.

For lack of anything better to do, she followed Melissa's car toward the center of town, finally passing it in front of Bodyworks when Melissa pulled over to park. A block later Diana honked at the crowd going into Dopey's, a local hangout, but her days of calorie-rich junk food were over. She had a goal, one she was determined to reach very soon. Instead of the burger stop, she pulled into the gas station on the corner and checked her reflection in the rearview mirror, while the attendant filled the tank.

"Pale as library paste," she muttered. She needed her California tan more than ever. It made her perfect complexion glow, and even if her father said it was unhealthy, it wouldn't kill her to tan up just for the next crucial week or so. She smiled, remembering the looks and wolf whistles she'd gotten after arriving from Santa Barbara.

When she'd paid with her mother's credit card, she continued the drive, wondering if Hope would go home after practice and play the violin tape. In the past Diana had stolen Hope's sheet music and sabotaged her boyfriend but now, maybe Hope would think she was trying to turn over a new leaf. People could change, couldn't they?

Ten minutes later, Diana entered the wide front doors of Pineland Spa and went directly to the front desk. "Tucker. We have a family membership and I'd like to use the tanning room, please." After signing the registration sheet, she put her hands in her lavender pockets and followed the attendant down the carpeted hallway.

"Now that's the kind of effort I like to see from the best squad in the region!" Coach Engborg said with a smile at the end of practice that day. "Honest to goodness sweat!"

Sean rolled onto his back and flung his limp arms onto the mat. "Slave driver! We haven't worked this hard since we were out at the lake last summer."

Their coach laughed. "It paid off then and it'll pay off now. You and Peter were perfectly synchronized with that split." She looked at each of them and clapped her hands together. "You'll be dismissed in a minute, but first, listen. You probably have an idea what this is all about. We need another cheerleader, as everyone agrees. The problem is coming up with a fair, quick way to choose an alternate. Frankly, I don't want to be put in the position of having to call a full tryout, since I'd have to see everyone with an interest — and that was close to a hundred last time. Agree so far?"

She waited while Tara glanced at Olivia and Hope looked at Sean; they nodded. "I could simply appoint someone, of course, someone who came close in the spring tryouts, but that wouldn't be fair to the others. Since there's not much left of the season, I've come up with a plan.

"I'm going to ask disinterested parties to judge with me, a panel of three. Pres Tilford was a cheerleader and knows what to look for, and he no longer has any connection with the school. I'll try him and a faculty member. I have in mind Nick Stewart from the math department. He doesn't coach, so he has no conflicts of interest, but he's one of the teachers who comes to most of the games — another one who, I think, would be a good judge of spirit and ability. With three of us, majority will rule, no tie votes."

Olivia raised her hand. "Then you are having tryouts?"

"In a manner of speaking. The position is just for the rest of the season, next year I'd like to see the alternate try out for the regular squad. I want an underclass student who, I hope, can add to the skills of the squad in the fall, but I want someone who hasn't tried out before. That cuts out all last year's kids, I know. I intend to ask Diana Tucker. She says she's already been a cheerleader and has the ability. In addition to her, I'll consider as many as five, no more."

The coach cleared her throat and had to repeat herself over the groans and gasps. "I know Diana has done some questionable things to get herself accepted in this school, but she's new and no one has done much to make her feel at home. Maybe this is the break she needs."

"She nearly ruined our mascot!" Tara said.

"I admit, she's gone about things wrong. Still, she created a wonderful wolf."

"Which Hope had to go and find after Diana stole it!" Peter added.

Ardith Engborg nodded. "She's not perfect and I'll consider others. I just want you all to know what I've decided. I want the squad to introduce the alternate at the Varsity-Alumni game a week from Saturday night. I'll line up the judges for a week from tomorrow, after school right here. Any of you may suggest someone as long as she or he fits the criteria. The final choice is out of your hands, though, even yours, Olivia, so no one can blame any of you when the choice is made." She smiled at the five doubtful expressions. "It's the best I can do under the circumstances. I think it'll all work out in the end, and we'll have a great new member."

"It won't work out. It will *be* the end if Diana's chosen," Tara said later as the group left the locker rooms for the parking lot.

Peter looked at her. "You must admit, if you didn't know Diana, she would seem perfect. She's got the looks and the body, and she knows all the moves."

Tara made a face at him. "You're not kidding she knows all the moves. I agree, though, nobody else comes close or they would have already tried out. She doesn't even have Mr. Stewart for a class; he'll think she's the perfect answer, if we don't watch out."

Peter smiled at Tara, feeling better than he had in days, despite the circumstances. Of all people to agree with him, he would never have expected Tara. As the squad split up in the dusky lot, even his watching Hope hurry along without him didn't hurt as much as it had. He glanced quickly around for Tony Pell's car and when he didn't see it, he went back to talking with Tara.

Hope wasn't expecting Tony. She was trying to catch up with Sean as he opened the door to his Fiero. When she smiled, he grinned back. "Need a lift?"

Hope tried to look cheerful. "Can you spare about half an hour?"

He tilted his head. "Kate's got a baby-sitting job today. You wouldn't by any chance be trying to come between us?"

Hope wrinkled her nose. "Sean Dubrow, all you and I have in common is this squad and you know it. Kate Harmon's the best thing that ever happened to you — but right now I need your help."

He grinned again. "I'm a sucker for a mystery."

She got into the car. "How about a musical — *My Fair Lady*?"

Sean started the engine and gave her a questioning glance. "What?"

"*My Fair Lady, Pygmalion*, the story of a girl taken from the slums of London and given speech lessons, etiquette, voice training, you name it. She fools everybody and becomes a member of London society."

"Hope, I've seen the movie, but what are you talking about? And by the way, where are we going?"

She pointed right as they left the parking lot. "Bodyworks at the end of Main Street, just before Dopey's."

"How about just after a quick burger at Dopey's?"

"Sean!"

"Okay, okay. I still say this is a mystery."

"Not for long. Park right there." She sat in silence, her stomach a knot of tension while Sean

47

eased the Fiero into a spot in front of the building.

"What the heck are we doing — "

"Shhhh." She took his arm, hurrying him up the stairs towards the practice rooms, but there were no drifting strains of ballet music. Her heart fell. But although she had no idea what Melissa's schedule was, she nevertheless kept tugging Sean along until they were outside the proper door. The lights were on, and the moment she spotted Melissa, she pulled Sean closer. "Grand jeté," she whispered. "She's doing an arabesque."

Hope was breathless, and even Sean gasped softly as Melissa, her legs fully extended in front and behind her, performed a delicate leap. She repeated the move, without music, landed lightly in her toe shoes, and then walked to the barre where she bent into a series of relaxing exercises.

"Impressive," Sean whispered. "Who is she and why, Ms. Chang, are we standing out here watching her?"

"Doesn't she look familiar?"

Sean looked again and then shook his head. "Not exactly my type, sorry. Besides, Kate takes all my attention now."

"Never mind. We're here because that's Melissa Brezneski and in the next week, we're going to make her into a cheerleader, *the* cheerleader who will make the judges' decision unanimous."

Sean's dark eyes widened as he looked again at the ballerina and then to Hope. "You're absolutely crazy," he said.

CHAPTER

5

Sean started to laugh. "You're serious!"

Hope put her hands on her hips. "Let me put it this way, Dubrow. Who would you rather lift in a cheer, Diana Tucker or Melissa Brezneski? Who would you rather catch after a double leap? Who would you rather make all your practice mistakes in front of, Melissa or Diana?"

"You made your point! But there's only a week." He looked back through the glass-paned door as Melissa bent into some simple pliés, moving from first to fifth position and then slowly swinging her leg.

At the sound of their muffled voices, she looked up and frowned, trying to recognize the faces from across the room. When she saw Hope, she relaxed and started toward the door, hesitating again when she realized who was standing next to her. Sean Dubrow, easily the best-looking boy in the senior class, had been watching, too! She took a deep breath and opened the door. Sean looked uncomfortable.

"I'm sorry," Hope said, "We were talking too loud."

"No, I'm all finished. James doesn't have karate today, I don't think."

"No, Sean and I were in the neighborhood and, uh, I wanted to show him where James's lessons are. Do you know Sean, Melissa?"

Melissa put out her hand. "I know who you are, of course. I'm Melissa Brezneski." She stammered when she said it and wished she were better about boys. She wished she weren't standing there in a worn-out leotard and unmatched legwarmers, and most of all she wished her tongue didn't feel like it had bandages wrapped around it. "Are you interested in karate?" Nobody was saying much of anything.

Sean looked at Hope and back. "Some. I might take it up after cheerleading's over. That was quite an arabesque you did a while ago."

She felt her cheeks grow hot, the color seeping right up along her neck. "You've been out here that long?"

Sean looked helplessly at Hope. "Well, we didn't want to interrupt you. No music?"

"I just turned it off."

"Right. Well, Hope, I guess that's about it." Sean smiled and turned to go.

Hope put her arm out as Sean started to turn. "Would you do another for us? Do you mind, Melissa?"

Melissa tried to settle the pounding in her chest

as she shook her head. "No, I don't mind. Arabesque," she said as she got into position. "First arabesque." She extended one leg out behind her and crossed her arms at the wrists. "Second," she called extending her arms. "Third." She brought her arms forward. "Would you like to see fondu and penché?" She looked at Sean.

Sean looked at Hope and then back to Melissa. "Penché? No, I don't think we have time. It was beautiful, though. Thanks."

Hope waved good-bye. "Do you dance regularly?"

Melissa shook her head. "There's no troupe in Tarenton, and I just do this for myself, really. I love the music, and it's kind of a family tradition, started by my grandmother."

"So you'd have some free time if you needed it?"

"Yes, I guess so. Why?"

"Why?" Hope repeated. "Because I'm having a pizza party tomorrow night. Just five till seven or so since it's a school night. No dates or anything, just some of my friends. It'll be over early in case you have to study. We'd love to have you come."

Sean was looking at Hope as if she had suddenly started speaking another language.

Melissa blinked. "Well, I guess so. Five o'clock?"

"Yes. Very casual." Hope gave Melissa directions to her house and then said her last good-bye before hurrying down the stairs with Sean in tow. When they were finally in the Fiero, Hope began to laugh. "Sean, you're about the color of a radish."

He shook his head and leaned his forehead on the steering wheel. "So was *she*! Hope, she's too shy and, I don't know, quiet, maybe. I can't believe you did that to me. I hardly know an arabesque from a twirly gig, and she'd probably rather be hiding under the bleachers than doing a handspring in the gym. What pizza party?" he added suddenly, easing the car from its parking spot.

"The pizza party where the entire squad gets to know Melissa and helps me convince her to try out for the alternate position."

"Well, at least you've talked to the others already. Was I the last one?"

Hope cleared her throat. "Not exactly. You're the first."

He made a choking noise and hit the brake. "Nobody else knows about this scheme but me?"

"Relax. I've got tonight and all day tomorrow to convince them. Do me a favor. Call Peter when you get home and explain. Better still, swing by his apartment after you drop me off. These things always work out better in person. Tell him how fabulously she moves. Tell him all we have to do is translate that arabesque into an aerial and a leap. Ballet dancers are superb athletes."

"Hope, Melissa might be in great shape, but she blends in with the lockers. What about charisma and spirit, all that quality stuff? She doesn't exactly shine, you know." He was still trying to talk her out of it when he pulled up in front of Hope's house.

Hope put her hand on the door handle. "No, she doesn't shine — yet. But by this time next week, she'll outshine everybody else because if she doesn't, your next partner on the gym floor will be — "

"I know, I know. The mean, loopy blonde from California. Okay, Hope, I'll do my best. So it's at five, tomorrow night?"

"Yes, five, and just to be safe, tell Peter I've called a meeting at lunch, too, just us in the corner by the water fountain. I'll tell everyone else on the squad and let them know."

Sean saluted. "Aye, aye, Captain."

At the sound of a car in her driveway, Jessica craned her neck. Daniel, she thought, already resenting the intrusion on her solitude. She'd turned on the lights, stuck her mother's casserole in the oven, and flipped the tape in the stereo.

"Hello, Jessica," Daniel called as he hung up his coat. He added something she couldn't hear over the music.

"What?" she called from the couch.

"Nothing!" He came into the room and turned down the stereo. "I just asked how your foot was doing. Can't you keep that down a little?"

"It's better, and there wasn't anybody home but me," she answered with forced pleasantness.

"Can I get you anything?"

She shook her head. "I'll wait for Mom." She'd probably hurt his feelings, but she wasn't in the mood for talking, especially just making polite conversation, which was all they did, anyway.

"Suit yourself. Dinner smells good. I'll eat later. I've got to go upstairs and change for basketball practice."

Jessica turned from her spot on the couch. "What basketball practice?"

"Didn't your mother tell you? I'm going to play on the Alumni team for the PTA game. I played on Varsity for three years at Tarenton. Of course, that was in the dark ages. The team's practicing every night in the Middle School gym." With that he waved and disappeared toward the stairs.

Jessica stared at the fashion magazine in her lap. Daniel Bennett, a starting basketball player? She couldn't imagine him as anything but a tall, thin computer whiz, and a not-very-interested stepfather. While he was changing, Jessica grappled with the idea that she'd be cheering for him. She groaned. He was too old, too boring, too totally wrong. She leaned against the back of the couch and stared at the ceiling. Alumni meant kids barely out of school, didn't it? People still in college, or working around town, who were Pres's age, or Patrick's, would be playing, not people Daniel's age. She'd have to cheer for her own stepfather! The rest of the squad would never let her hear the end of it.

Her thoughts were interrupted by a second voice, this time her mother's. "Daniel home? I saw his car outside."

Jessica waited for her mother to cross the room. "He's upstairs getting dressed for basketball practice. Why didn't you tell me?"

Abby Bennett took off her coat. "Tell you? Oh, I guess I forgot, what with your foot and everything. That's the night he decided to play, and there was so much excitement with you. . . . I'm sorry, Jessica, it slipped my mind." The phone rang in the kitchen and she left to answer it, returning moments later.

"That was Patrick. He was calling from a phone booth and said to tell you that the delivery van for Tarenton Furniture broke down. They've hired Patrick to make the delivery tonight. He just sent Tony Pell home so he's driving himself. He's delivering couches to Marshfield, it seems. He'll catch up with you after school tomorrow, if he gets a break." She looked at the disappointment on her daughter's face. "Jessica, darling, Patrick has a real job, with real responsibility."

Jessica closed her eyes and nodded, but misery washed over her. Maybe she was just a high school senior, but everything she felt was real, too, crushingly, hopelessly real, and the one person who might understand was driving away from her with a truckful of furniture.

Tarenton High School divided its homerooms alphabetically and Room One for the junior class included Melissa Brezneski and Hope Chang. From her seat by the windows, Melissa looked at Hope, admiring her dark hair and pretty, perfect features. She didn't seem like the type to give parties in the middle of the week, Melissa thought, but then again, she hadn't seemed like the type to get herself all mixed up in the excitement surrounding Tony Pell and a foiled robbery. It had been the talk of the school, and if Hope seemed quiet and studious before, she sure had a new image now.

For Hope's part, she'd spent the better part of

the morning fighting her own set of heart palpitations and stomach butterflies. What had she done, she kept asking herself. First she had to convince everybody on the squad that Melissa could be made into a cheerleader, and then she had to convince Melissa.

It seemed that lunch period would never arrive, but when it did her anxiety got worse. She was the last one of the group to get a tray and make it to the table. She approached with a smile, however. Every one of the squad who was dating steadily had somebody from outside Tarenton High. Tony was in her own life at the moment, Sean had Kate, Olivia was with David Duffy, and Jessica, of course, had Patrick. None of them had been included in the pizza party tonight, and every cheerleader was waiting for an explanation — all except Sean and Peter, who had decided to leave it to Hope.

She sat down and waited for Peter to take a swallow from his milk carton.

"What gives?" Tara asked from her spot next to him.

"This had better be good," Olivia added.

Sean grinned at all of them. "It is. Tell them, Hope, so I'm not the only one who thinks you've gone bananas."

Hope cleared her throat, finding the words she'd been up half the night rehearsing. "I've found our next cheerleader. It'll take some work, but I *know* she'll be absolutely perfect once we — well, once we loosen her up a little. Once we. . . ." Hope found herself groping for words.

"Once we turn the caterpillar into a butterfly!" Sean added.

Tara pointed her half-eaten sandwich at Hope. "Could you get to the point before I get to dessert?"

Hope glared at her. "The point is that Diana Tucker will get the position if we don't do something. She's a natural, whether we like it or not. Think about it. She's already been a cheerleader, she can do anything we can do. She'd love to get on the squad. Just look how hard she's tried. Sabotage and dirty tricks haven't worked, so now she's turning sweet." For evidence, Hope pulled the Perlman tape from her purse. "A gift to me."

"She's been carrying my books every chance she gets," Jessica added.

"She practically cried on my shoulder with sympathy the night you fell," Peter told Jessica.

"*There's* proof," Hope broke in, "and don't forget that we won't be judging, either. Not one of us has a say in it. Mark my words, she's pulling the same sweetness-and-light routine on Coach."

Olivia's shoulders slumped. "But there's nobody else. Anyone who knows the moves or has the ability either tried out last year or is already on another team."

"Not everybody."

Five expectant faces waited for Hope to continue. Her heart was pumping furiously as she found her enthusiasm again. "What we need to do is find one person, an athlete with superb coordination, and make her into the challenger. And I've found her. I've thought it through a thousand times. If we can't agree, and we come up with different choices, it'll never work. We need all our effort and energy behind one person. I've found her and she's got everything it takes."

"And this mystery girl agrees?" Tara asked.

Hope's smile was a little forced. "Well — "

"Not exactly," Sean broke in.

Jessica looked at him. "What do you mean, not exactly?"

"She doesn't exactly know anything about the plan, *yet*. But she's perfect. I think," he added hastily, with a quick glance at Hope.

Olivia was trying to talk around her mouthful of hamburger. "Who is this cheerleader-in-the-rough?"

"Melissa Brezneski," Hope said.

Tara and Olivia said, "Who?" Jessica said, "What!" and Peter just sighed, having already listened to Sean's pep talk the night before.

"Melissa Brezneski. Tonight at my house we're *all* going to convince her that what she wants more than anything else in the world is to join our squad, and then all of us are going to make it happen. That's why I'm having the pizza party."

"With no dates," Olivia muttered.

"This is hardly the time for romance," Hope said. "Melissa is an awesome ballerina. She has the ability to translate that into cheerleading."

Tara looked hopeful. "Well, at least she's used to performing in front of crowds, then, if she's in a ballet company."

Sean cleared his throat. "Not exactly."

"Here we go again!" Tara muttered.

"I mean, she just dances for herself, mostly. But

58

it's terrific, anyway, really," he added, looking from one doubtful expression to the next. "I saw her yesterday at Bodyworks." He tried to forget the way Melissa had blushed when she'd discovered they'd been watching. There wasn't any point in being negative, not if he wanted to cheer with someone besides the terror from Santa Barbara.

While everyone was groaning, Peter thought to ask what she looked like. Jessica scanned the cafeteria. "Over there, putting her tray back."

Tara knitted her brow. "The only girl putting her tray back has her hair in a bun and has on — what is that? — a brown man's shirt and maroon toreador pants."

"Trust me." Hope smiled as she looked at their incredulous expressions. "She's our answer."

CHAPTER

The dismissal bell rang shrilly as Mary Ellen entered the small office connected to the Garrison High gymnasium. She'd changed into warm-ups and pulled her hair into a no-nonsense clasp, and as she looked at her clipboard she laughed at herself, feeling as though she were imitating Coach Engborg.

Then she took a deep breath and went onto the gym floor to give the waiting squad her brightest smile.

Garrison had six cheerleaders, three boys and three girls. Mary Ellen looked at each of them, quickly reviewing their names in her head. The boys were easy. The captain was a redhead, Rusty O'Connor, equal in height to fellow senior David Dennison, a brunet. Red Rusty and dark David, Mary Ellen memorized. Andrea Hamel and Martha Guccione were the senior girls, and the juniors were Eric Smith and Andrea's sister, Amy.

Rusty, David, Eric, Andrea, Martha, and *Amy*. Mary Ellen wished they'd smile back.

"Let's get to work," Mary Ellen said cheerfully, hustling them over to the mini-trampoline. With each girl having a boy for support, the Garrison cheers were designed differently, relying more heavily on lifts and maneuvers requiring strength; it was these she intended to review once they warmed up.

"Jumping jacks," Mary Ellen called out first as the six began their calisthenics. They did them perfectly without complaint but without enthusiasm, either. When they'd finished, Mary Ellen called them back to the bleachers but decided against a peptalk.

"Andrea, would you please demonstrate your favorite cheer, and when she's finished, Rusty, show us your least favorite."

She ignored the look the two gave each other and concentrated on the layout of the moves. When they'd finished, she looked at the whole group. "Let's think about why Andrea's works so well."

David shrugged his shoulders. "It fires up the fans. It's simple, two cartwheels and a kick line."

"It's easy and it works every time," Amy added.

Mary Ellen nodded. "Now, Rusty, let's talk about the one you chose. It looked much more complicated."

"Yeah, it is. It's really impressive with the aerials and jumps, but the timing's tough to remember, which throws off the words sometimes."

Mary Ellen hoped they could see her point. "Maybe, then, the easiest ones are the best to use.

The fans like them because they can remember the words; you like them because they're peppy and fast. They work, right?" She waited while each of the cheerleaders nodded. "That should tell you — that should tell *us* — something. For today let's concentrate on what you think are the five best and simplest cheers, and make them perfect before the next game."

The new coach got the cheerleaders back on the floor and then watched as they went through their paces. There was still hesitation in each of them, and finally Eric dropped his arms. "It feels weird, you know, showing you our cheers."

Rusty nodded. "Last year you and I cheered against each other. I feel like I'm giving out secret information, Mary El — I mean, Coach Tilford."

Mary Ellen took a deep breath. "I'm not the enemy. I'm here because I want to coach. I love it and I want you to be fantastic."

"Yeah, the second best team in the league," somebody whispered, but when Mary Ellen turned to look, nobody said anything more.

"Stick to what you know and make it perfect," she told them, glancing at the clock as the minutes dragged by.

At four-forty-five, Mrs. Brezneski went out to start the car. As Melissa slid into the passenger seat, her mother smiled at her. "Now, Missy, you just give me a call when you need a ride home, unless one of the other kids offers."

One of the others. . . . Melissa nodded, hating to be driven to a party by her mother, but having no other way of getting to Hope's. Her mother

needed the car tonight. "I may not know anybody, I don't even know who's going to be there
except Hope and Sean."

"Well, enjoy yourself. Hope would make a nice
friend."

Melissa barely heard her mother's conversation
as they headed for the Chang's neighborhood. Her
mother was always commenting on her classmates, saying cheerful things like that, intimating
that Melissa needed more friends. In Melissa's
heart she knew it was true, but parents never
understood how tough that was. You couldn't
just walk up to someone like a nerd and say, "Hi,
want to be friends?" She didn't go out for sports
and except for the yearbook committee, she
wasn't in any school clubs. She liked Hope,
though. Besides homeroom, they shared a few
classes every year. Hope was never afraid to talk
about her love of classical music or anything else
that most people thought was weird. Hope was
a brain and she was proud of it!

I'm a brain, too, Melissa thought. But unlike
Hope, she hated it when the teachers repeatedly
asked her the answers to questions, especially
when one of the boys in her class had already
given a wrong reply. Ballet was her life. Music
and motion took her away and gave her time for
daydreams, a place where she could imagine she
was dancing with Mikhail Baryshnikov.

"Here we are," her mother said, shaking her
from her reverie. Melissa's stomach immediately
flipped and she crossed her arms against her waist.

"Thanks. See you later," she replied, getting out
of the car with an anxious glance at the ones

parked at the curb. There was a red Fiero and an old green Ford. Good, she thought, not too many kids. She wasn't too terrific in crowds.

Melissa walked up the brick path and wished her mother would drive away instead of waiting till she was inside. She looked at her pants and stuffed her gloved hands into her pockets. She'd probably dressed all wrong. She should have asked Hope what to wear, but it was too embarrassing. Maybe to Hope's friends casual meant long skirts or warm-ups. Why hadn't she asked? Why hadn't she found out who would be there? Why hadn't she stayed home?

The front door opened before she could knock. "You must be Melissa Brezneski. I'm Caroline Chang, Hope's mother. Please come in." Melissa shook hands and stepped over the threshold.

"Melissa! We're so glad you could come," Hope called from behind her mother. "Come on in the kitchen. You're just in time to put in an order. How do you like your pizza?"

Melissa blinked as she followed Hope through the modern house, unbuttoning her parka as she went. "Hot, I guess." Hope laughed and it made her feel good. "Mushrooms and pepperoni." The two girls entered the kitchen and Melissa was aware of a sea of faces looking at her. She concentrated on James, however, Hope's younger brother, who took her coat and gloves.

"How's karate going?"

"Awesome," he answered. "Hope says if I take care of everybody's jackets, I get all the pizza I can eat, as long as I stay out of the way."

Melissa smiled. "That seems fair enough."

Hope tugged her elbow and she stepped farther into the group as the hostess looked from her to everybody else. It was a relief to see that the girls all wore jeans or pleated pants like hers.

"Melissa, you know Jessica. How about Tara Armstrong, Olivia Evans, and this is Peter Rayman, and of course, Sean."

"Hi," was all she could manage as they stared at her. At least it felt like staring. "Okay, Melissa, you get first choice," said Sean.

"Mushroom and pepperoni," she repeated.

"Excellent choice," he replied, giving her a friendly grin. Sean finally picked up the phone.

The others gave their orders before Hope shepherded everyone into the family room. It was large and full of paintings, the outside wall given over to a brick fireplace with a raised hearth. Melissa watched Peter sit by the fire, and tried to ignore the feeling that Tara was staring at her hair and that Olivia seemed very interested in her man-sized sweater. At the last minute, she'd tied one of her sisters bandannas around her narrow waist. Maybe it looked stupid. The room was too quiet.

"Music," Jessica said. "Peter, get a tape going."

Sean came into the room. "All set. The Pizza Palace says twenty minutes. I guess you've met everybody, Melissa."

She nodded. They were all familiar to her, but it seemed a little unbalanced if everyone had arrived. She looked at Sean. "Aren't you all part of the — "

"Great sweater," Olivia blurted out. "I bet it's from Marnie's."

Melissa turned to look at her. "Yes, I got it for Christmas. I wasn't too sure I liked the pink and blue together."

"Great combination," Olivia said. "And your hair, I like the way it's pulled back. How long is it?"

"Nearly to my waist."

"Your waist!" Olivia looked at Hope.

The room seemed tense; they were all waiting for something — something more than pizza, Melissa thought. She caught Peter watching her from the hearth, but when she looked back, he stirred the embers.

"This is the cheerleading squad," Melissa said as much to herself as to the others, but they were instantly quiet. Jessica looked at Tara. Olivia looked at Sean. Peter kept stirring, and Hope asked that the music be turned down.

"Aren't you?"

"We sure are," Sean replied, "and we think you ought to join us."

Melissa's dark brown eyes widened as she looked at the senior. "I don't understand."

"Maybe you better sit down. Maybe we all better sit down," Hope said, shooing the group onto the couch and surrounding rug. She offered Melissa a spot in the easy chair. The ballerina sat down slowly, feeling like a biology specimen pinned to a board. If she'd had a few butterflies in her stomach when she'd arrived, they'd multiplied into an entire herd under her ribs.

Hope was giving each of them stern looks and then she cleared her throat. "Coach Engborg has decided that our squad needs an alternate

66

member, Melissa, somebody who'll practice with us, and be ready to take over if one of the regular members is out."

Jessica raised her crutches and everybody smiled. "The season's practically over and the position's just till tryouts at the end of the year."

Melissa closed her eyes and laughed. "Coach would never want me. I'm in her gym class and she barely knows I'm alive. I don't even look like any of you. She'd never appoint me."

Peter elbowed Hope. "It's not exactly an appointment. There'll be one quick tryout."

"Very quick," Jessica added.

"Couple of minutes after school next week," Sean threw in.

"Tryouts? Next week?" Melissa shook her head. "No, I don't think so. This isn't my thing, not by a mile. There must be hundreds of girls who would die for a chance to cheer with you." As she said it she looked at Peter and felt the awful flush creeping up from her turtleneck jersey.

Sean put his hand on her shoulder. "You're perfect. I watched you dance yesterday," he said quietly.

The flush only got worse. She looked from one senior boy to the other. She knew Sean Dubrow only as the flashy guy who was always wisecracking in the halls, so sure of himself he'd tried out for the Young Mr. Tarenton contest. She thought he might be teasing, and it added to her confusion.

"Hope, I'm really sorry. I guess that's why you asked me over tonight, why you thought you had to have me here for pizza or something. I don't want to be a cheerleader. I couldn't, really. I can't imagine why you'd even think of me. If you need somebody in a hurry, you know who would be perfect? The new girl from California, Diana Tucker. Cheerleading is all she ever talks about. You should have had her come over here." Melissa got up from the chair and looked around for her parka. Inside, her emotions were doing handsprings. Part of her felt crushed that Hope's invitation was only because they wanted something from her, but part of her was thrilled to have been asked.

"Really, Diana Tucker's the one."

Six people groaned in unison.

Sean wasn't sure what to do, but he knew one thing for sure. If they let Melissa Brezneski leave now, she'd never agree and he'd spend the rest of the season with Diana too close for comfort. "Pizza time," he yelled out as he heard the back door open and close and sure enough, nine-year-old James came into the room, balancing the wide cardboard boxes. Sean was still standing next to Melissa, and he tapped her shoulder a second time. "Come on, you have to eat."

"Pepperoni and mushroom," Tara said, as she opened a box and put it on the coffee table.

Hope walked over next to Sean. "Melissa, I invited you here to meet my friends and have some supper. We'd like you to stay."

Melissa hesitated. Did they look sincere or desperate? The room smelled wonderfully of tomato sauce and mozzarella. Her stomach growled.

"There's your answer," Hope laughed. "Your stomach's saying, 'Stay and feed me.'"

"And so's mine," Peter added. He lifted out the first slice and offered it. Reluctantly, Melissa took it from him and he was surprised to feel a tug in his chest. He was touched by the shy way she'd tried to figure out what they were up to. We're ganging up on her, he thought. I'd be a wreck, too, if this bunch pounced on me out of the blue.

Melissa was cute. Not in the way Tara was or even Jessica, but in a quiet way, as if she just kept it to herself. Peter knew plenty of shy girls, but most of them were awkward or tongue-tied. Melissa sort of drifted into the room and watched or listened to everyone else, as if trying to decide whether the group was serious or teasing. She had a way of tilting her head when she listened, a way he liked. He agreed with Hope; underneath her plain exterior, he could see glimpses of the Melissa Brezneski that Sean had watched through the door of the Bodyworks practice room. If they didn't give up on her, that other Melissa might break through in time to save them all.

The mood brightened as they ate and the conversation drifted away from cheerleading. Finally, over dishes of double dutch chocolate ice cream, Jessica leaned forward. "I was telling everybody about your history report. That was some story about Warsaw and your grandmother."

Melissa looked hesitant, but smiled. "It's all true. When I was little, I thought the only thing I wanted to do in the world was become a ballerina. Her stories about Poland and the grand house and hotels and the orchestras. . . . Of course, I'll never be good enough, but I still love to practice and I'll always love music." Everyone was listening and she stopped. "Of course *Swan Lake* and *Romeo and Juliet* aren't exactly Huey Lewis or Tina Turner."

"Or even the Police," Hope added playfully. "Nice change of pace, though, right Melissa?"

"Yes, I guess so."

"Cheerleading's not all that different from ballet," Olivia said, looking quickly at Hope. "The moves are, but you're in better shape than any of us, most likely. All that leaping and spinning and positions at the barre keep you in great shape. It might be fun to come to the gym some afternoon and show us a leap."

"It's called an arabesque," Sean corrected, and grinned as Olivia arched her eyebrows in surprise.

"Arabesque, excuse me. You could do a few and compare them to what we do."

"In order to see if I'm good enough for the squad?" Melissa shook her head. "I'm not. I know what you're trying to do, but believe me, I *can't* cheer in front of the student body while they scream for the players."

"They'd cheer for sure if you did," Sean replied, almost laughing at Melissa's startled, doe-eyed expression.

It was nearly seven and Hope didn't want any of them to start up again. They'd put enough pressure on Melissa for one night. She went to the stereo, dropped in a tape, and waited. As the violin strains began, accompanied by a full orchestra, everyone turned to look at her. "Itzhak

70

Perlman playing Beethoven's 'Concerto in D.' Diana gave it to me because she likes me so much. She'll get each of us before the week's out, I can guarantee it."

Melissa gave Sean a quizzical expression. "Never mind," he said. "Just think long and hard about dropping by the gym after school, soon."

The party broke up as Patrick arrived for Jessica. After being introduced to Melissa he helped Jessica with her jacket. "Henley's Transport Service here for the precious cargo."

Jessica pointed a crutch at him. "I'm the only person in the room who gets compared to a priceless vase."

Patrick laughed as they headed for the kitchen door. "Just be glad I didn't pack you up in newspaper and bubbled plastic before I put you in the van."

Melissa laughed with everyone else, grateful that the subject had changed at last. As they stood in the kitchen, she asked Hope if she could use the phone.

"If that's for a ride, forget it," a deep voice said behind her. "Henley Transport may have just left, but you still get to choose between Rayman Taxi and Dubrow Chauffeur Service." Sean was still grinning that grin of his.

"One's as bad as the other," Tara said, elbowing Peter. "I'm with Dubrow."

Sean dug into his pocket. "I can settle this. Heads it's me, tails, you get Peter."

"I don't really think — "

"Too late," Sean chortled, already flipping his quarter into the air. He slapped the coin on the

71

back of his hand and looked. "Tails. Peter, you win."

Melissa hurried into her parka as everyone gathered purses, backpacks, and jackets, sure she was the only one whose heart was hammering. It made it tough to breath evenly, and she was afraid she'd blush again. Nevertheless, Melissa found herself saying thank you, following the others, and hurrying out into the cold toward the cars at the curb. It wasn't until Olivia, Tara, and Sean called good-bye that she realized nobody else was going with Peter.

"Take care, Rayman," Sean called as he opened his own car. "Take care of our ballerina."

CHAPTER

"I will absolutely die if he plays on the Alumni team," Jessica said, as Patrick pulled the moving van into her driveway.

"Maybe he's still a good player. Maybe he'll be the star shot, Jessica," Patrick replied as he hugged her.

Jessica closed her eyes. "That would be worse! How will I ever live this down? My own stepfather. . . . I have to cheer for my own stepfather!"

"You could always hurt your other ankle."

Jessica raised her head and stared at Patrick in the light from the back porch. "You think it's all a big joke. You don't even care!"

Patrick shook his head. "Jessica, of course I care. I care about what you're feeling, but it's just a fund-raising game. It's supposed to be fun, not a big deal."

She sighed and opened her door. "And I'm just a dumb cheerleader making a mountain out of a molehill."

Patrick came around to her side and matched her slow pace to the door. "You're not dumb."

"But the rest of it?"

He jammed his hands into his jacket pockets. "Forget it. I've got a lot on my mind and I don't want to argue." He sighed as they reached the door. He kissed her, but there wasn't much feeling between them. "Jessica, nobody will think anything about it, if you don't. Treat it like the good time it's supposed to be."

"So I don't bug you with my problems."

"I'm sorry. If you're really upset, why don't you talk to one of the other cheerleaders? Olivia would understand, or Tara."

"Maybe I will," she muttered. Without another kiss, she went into her house, feeling like a balloon had burst or worse, had sprung a slow leak. She'd waited for two days to see Patrick and pour her heart out, and now he was too busy to care. She came into the house and hung up her jacket, listening to the voices of Daniel and her mother over their late dinner in the dining room. Without calling hello, she went up the stairs to her room.

Melissa told her anxious parents that the pizza party had been fun, mentioned the possibility of a history test, and went up to her room. She didn't study, however; she stretched out on her bed, hugged a pillow, put on a Whitney Houston tape, and stared at the magazine cutouts and posters of Mikhail Baryshnikov and Maria Tallchief on her bulletin board.

Melissa's throat felt as though marshmallows were stuck in it; she was so close to tears she had to blink. Peter Rayman, with his sandy hair and soft eyes, had talked about cheerleading all the way home, how different the members were from each other, the good times they had together, and the fights, too. It wasn't until they'd reached her house that he brought up the subject of her joining the squad. "Just think about it; we'll give you all the help you need," he'd said.

"Why me?" she whispered now, alone in her room. She was all wrong, and she knew it even if they didn't. She'd never make it through a try-out in front of Coach Engborg in a week. No way. Then they'd be disappointed and she'd have let them down. Olivia, Tara, Hope, and Jessica were one thing, but Sean and Peter? How could she ever relax enough to cheer with two boys there? Ridiculous! The whole idea was too dumb to think about.

"Missy, I need some notebook paper." The sound of her sister's voice made her sit up. Molly Brezneski, a Tarenton High sophomore, was already heading for the desk in the corner. When she'd grabbed a handful she turned around and grinned. "So, who's the guy who drove you home in the green car?"

"Spy!"

"Come on, my room's right over the driveway. All I could see was his parka sleeve. Were you out with a *boy*?"

"No. I was at Hope Chang's for pizza and Peter Rayman drove me home, that's all."

"Peter Rayman! That's all!"

Melissa started to laugh. "You know Peter?"

Molly groaned. She was always groaning at her older sister's lack of interest in Tarenton High School life. "He's a cheerleader and a senior — everybody knows Peter Rayman. Everybody knows Hope, for that matter. Who else was there?"

"Molly, mind your own business for once, okay?"

"Any other cheerleaders? How about Sean Dubrow? He's sooooooo gorgeous."

"Sean was there."

"Awesome!"

"Calm down." She laughed. "It wasn't awesome, it was just pizza with the cheerleaders."

Molly's eyes, as big and brown as her sister's, were now as wide with surprise as Melissa's had been earlier. "Wait a minute. How can you just sit there on your bed and tell me you had pizza with the cheerleaders and Peter drove you home and you probably even talked to Sean? What did he say? Every word! Why aren't you screaming and calling a million friends to tell them?"

"I don't want anyone to know. They invited me because they tried to talk me into joining the squad."

"What?" Molly did the screaming and sank onto the bed next to her sister.

"Will you please calm down?" Melissa hissed. "I told them I wasn't interested. Be careful, you're scrunching the paper you just borrowed."

"Nooo," Molly groaned. "Let me get this straight. The entire cheerleading squad invited you to Hope's, asked you to join them, and you said no? You said no and Peter Rayman still drove you home?"

"Yes."

"Melissa, you are absolutely crazy. How could you?"

Melissa sighed. "You wouldn't understand."

"Mulled cider," Pres said, raising two mugs as Mary Ellen came into their house, from a visit with her family.

Mary Ellen smiled. She hung up her coat, kicked off her boots, and hurried to the warmth of the fire.

"Gemma asked me if I felt like a traitor working with the Garrison squad. Her friends are teasing her about it. Nobody understands; not my own little sister, Gemma; not the old squad; not the new ones, either. Pres, even the Garrison cheerleaders are self-conscious in front of me." She rubbed her forehead. "I had no idea it would be this tough."

"It's just a temporary assignment," he reminded her. "You're the one who keeps telling me it's worth the effort."

"Some days I just don't think so anymore. Never mind. Tell me something that will cheer me up."

Pres watched as the firelight reflected on her golden hair and he kissed her tenderly. "I made a meatloaf for tomorrow night so neither of us has to cook. How's that for a man who never lifted a spoon in a kitchen before he married?"

Mary Ellen laughed. "Not bad for starters."

"Coach Engborg called. She asked how you were doing, of course, but she also asked if I'd judge a tryout session for an alternate cheerleader. She wants Nick Stewart and me next Thursday afternoon."

"No kidding! It's about time Tarenton got around to an alternate. It's a shame Jessica's fall forced the issue."

"She also wanted to remind you that practice for the alumni cheerleading squad starts tomorrow night in the Middle School gym. And one particular cheerleader asked to be excused from practice, but she'll make the game. She's flying in for the weekend from Providence, Rhode Island."

"Nancy Goldstein! She's coming back from Brown? Fantastic!"

Pres was happy to see real enthusiasm return to Mary Ellen. "Just for the weekend; she says she took too much time off from classes when I was in the hospital to stay any longer than that. I have a sneaking suspicion it's the game *and* my fellow judge bringing her back."

"She and Nick really hit it off, didn't they? Great news. Maybe Nancy can give me some advice about Garrison." Mary Ellen felt one hundred percent better. One of her best friends and former squad member would be back to cheer with her; the game promised to be a hilarious evening and love was in the air. She kissed Pres. Maybe life was looking up after all.

The following morning Coach Engborg signaled for Diana from the other end of the hall and the blonde junior rushed through the throng of students, knowing it could only mean one thing.

"Diana," the coach began, "I wanted to talk to you about the alternate cheerleader position. Next Thursday afternoon I'm going to see a few interested underclass students try out. The spot's open for the rest of the season. I've mentioned it to Heather Mazanec, a sophomore who cheers for the Independent Football League, and she's mentioned Andrew Taylor. I know how interested you are, so I hope you'll give it a try as well."

Diana felt her face redden. "Give it a try! Coach, this was all my idea. Why do you need anybody besides me?"

Coach Engborg looked surprised. "Diana, I agreed with your suggestion, of course, but I'd already discussed it in detail with the principal before I ran into you. I'm the coach. It would hardly be fair if I just picked my own choice."

"Then I *am* your choice?"

The coach sighed. "Diana, I think you have the ability, and I'd like to see you at the tryouts Thursday afternoon. There'll be three judges. I'm asking that each of you prepare 'Give Me a T,' which you'll do together, and then two of your own choice, which each of you will perform individually. Of course, if you'd rather not — "

"Of course I'll be there! The others will be wasting their time, that's all," she replied irritably. The look on the coach's face told her she'd gone too far and she sweetened her tone. "Being on the squad, even as a alternate, would give me a chance to get to know the kids better, maybe make up for trying to mess up the mascot." Diana hoped she looked properly repentant. "You can count on me, Coach Engborg!"

For the first time since she could remember, Melissa found herself daydreaming in class. She was distracted by the least thing. In history, Troy Fredericks' shoulder seemed closer than usual. She looked at the back of his head and envisioned him making a foul shot while the stands were hushed. She was sitting on the first row of the bleachers with the cheerleaders. . . . Crazy! It was too crazy to think about.

Hope had left homeroom with Melissa and then caught up with her later in the hall, talking about Tony and an upcoming violin recital. They parted at the stairs as she mentioned a tape of *The Nutcracker* she wanted to rent from the video store. Melissa watched her disappear up the staircase. Hope was easy to talk to. Could they still be friends if Melissa didn't try out?

Melissa had left history as Diana hurried to Jessica to carry her books as usual. Melissa wondered why the squad didn't offer their help to the most obvious choice. Diana was so pretty and so interested. Jessica caught Melissa's eye. Read my expression, she thought. We want you, Melissa, not the sneaky, petty, jealous girl next to me.

Between third and fourth periods Sean fell into step with Peter on their way up to physics.

"I'm telling you, Dubrow, it's hopeless. I drove her home, I should know. Melissa's not going to change her mind; I don't know what you and Hope expected. You can't gang up on somebody and force her into becoming something she's not.

I know exactly how she feels, even if you don't. Hope talked me into that stupid Young Mr. Tarenton Contest. Melissa probably feels just the way I did. At least she's had the good sense to turn us down from the beginning. We should leave her alone."

Sean shook his head. He and Peter were different as night and day, and now was one of those times when it showed. "Maybe she doesn't want to be left alone. Come on, man, I know about girls." As he talked, he spotted Diana Tucker coming down the stairs toward them. It made him more determined than ever. "Melissa's shy; she's got talent, untapped talent. I've seen that much with my own eyes. I'm not giving up. In fact, Rayman, I'll bet you a Deluxe at Dopey's, giant shake included, that if you and I work on her, we can get her to try out. Is it a bet?"

"Hi, boys, what's the bet? Trying to get another unsuspecting girl to go out?"

Sean looked at Diana's penetrating blue eyes. It was as good a lie as any. "Sure, Diana. Peter's bet me a Deluxe at Dopey's that we can have half the senior class in love with us by graduation."

Diana batted her eyelashes. "Gee, Sean, I hope you'll save some time to give me a hand in chemistry. I'm just lost." She sauntered away.

Sean muttered, "Over my dead body."

Peter shook his head. "I hate to say it, but this is one bet I hope you win. I'll give you all the help I can as long as we don't do anything to hurt Melissa."

At four-thirty Olivia and Tara sat next to each

other on the gym floor, massaging their calf muscles. Coach had doubled their Thursday practice session for the game the following night, their first without Jessica and one of two scheduled before the Alumni-Varsity Game.

"It's just as well that Melissa turned us down," Olivia said. "How would we ever have the time to work with her and practice and do homework?"

Tara leaned back on her elbows. "I guess we'd just have to give up homework."

"That would be a dream come true," Hope replied, getting to her feet. "I have to squeeze in violin practice, too."

As Ardith Engborg dismissed them and left for her office, they all looked at each other. "Anybody talk to Melissa today about tryouts?" Hope asked.

"I stood next to her in the lunch line," Olivia said. "I brought up ballet and the game and everything else I could think of so she'd say something, but she didn't."

"Of course she didn't," Peter answered. "We're not letting her breathe."

Sean looked disgusted. "He's got it in his head that we're pushing too much."

"Maybe you're the problem," Tara said. "Of course, we girls know you two boys are just normal, boring, okay-looking guys. But some girls, especially underclass students, might think you're cute. They might be intimidated by senior, male cheerleaders. Peter Rayman and Sean Dubrow might be our biggest problem."

Sean looked at Peter. "I think that was a compliment."

"You're the one with the reputation, Dubrow, not me. Although, come to think of it, she wasn't very relaxed when I drove her home last night."

"You see? If she dates, it can't be very often. I've never seen her at any of the hangouts or school dances."

Hope looked discouraged. "I never should have dragged Sean to Bodyworks."

"Boy, is this flattering," Sean replied. "There's nothing like a trail of broken hearts to build a guy's confidence."

Tara pushed him playfully. "Where's Kate when we need her? She'd give you a good punch in the ribs for that!"

They all started glumly for the locker rooms. "What we need is time for her to get to know us," Hope said. "The one thing we don't have."

Sean pulled open the boys' locker room door. "What's the worst thing that could happen if we pressure her some more? She'd hate us for it and we'd be no worse off and neither would she."

Olivia made a face at him. "You can be totally gross, Sean. Don't you ever care about people's feelings?"

"Hey," he answered quickly, "I meant we might help her. Even if she doesn't become a cheerleader, it might bring her out of her shell."

Peter stepped past him. "I don't even want to hear what you've got in mind."

"Sure you do. Kate's coming to the game tomorrow night and you and I are going to double date." Sean glanced at Olivia, Hope, and Tara. "Sorry, ladies, this is mantalk. Can't give away all my secrets, now, can I?"

CHAPTER

The five best cheers on which the Garrison squad had chosen to concentrate were polished and perfect after less than an hour's practice. Their Friday night game was against St. Cloud in the Garrison gym. "You all look excellent," Mary Ellen told them as she blew her whistle.

"Sure we do," Andrea Hamel replied. "We can do these in our sleep."

"Tomorrow night I expect you to be wide awake!" Mary Ellen replied with a grin, but the joke fell flat. Rusty and David did a few deep knee bends; Eric and Martha stretched. It was Amy who finally spoke.

"Coach Tilford, if we're that good, can we go now? I've got a paper to write."

Mary Ellen looked at the clock. "Now? I guess so. How about putting in half an hour tomorrow before the game?"

Amy and Martha looked at each other. "We

never practice before a game. We have to eat and get ready, you know."

Mary Ellen certainly knew what was required before a game. She knew about the tension and preparations, but she caught herself before she made a hasty reply. "All right, then, as long as you promise to be perfect and see that Garrison wins, you're excused."

"It's okay if Garrison wins, as long as we're not playing Tarenton," Eric said under his breath as the squad walked past her. Mary Ellen was so tired of snide remarks she was tempted to blow the whistle again and march them all back onto the mats. However, she didn't, for one good reason. She wanted to go home as badly as they did. Tonight as she got ready to leave, she found herself contemplating the fact that she might have made a huge mistake in agreeing to help the Garrison squad.

"You promised!" Jessica Bennett knew she sounded like a spoiled child, but she could hardly believe Patrick's words, and he wasn't even talking to her in person. From her spot on the couch, she stared into the phone receiver as if she hadn't heard correctly.

Patrick sighed. "I know how you feel, Jessica. I want to go to the game as much as you do. I've hardly missed one, but this is business. It can't be helped. We took on the Tarenton Furniture account, and that means I have to work. It's as simple as that. I'll have Tony with me, if that helps any. Hope's in the same boat you are."

Hope wouldn't mind nearly as much, Jessica

thought. Hope was dating Tony for fun. There wasn't anything serious between them. It wasn't the same thing, not by a mile.

"Tell me you understand, Jessica," Patrick said softly. "It means a lot. I don't want to work on a Friday night, either. Did you ever think about that?"

"No," she sighed. "Never mind, then. Do what you have to do. I hope you make a ton of money."

Patrick laughed. "It has more to do with building up my professional reputation than making a ton of money. I want to make my living in this area, Jessica, and an account like Tarenton Furniture can make a huge difference. I'm sorry, I'll miss you."

"Well, I'll miss you, too," she replied as she hung up.

Daniel Bennett came into the room as she put the phone back on the table. His face was flushed from basketball practice, but he looked excited, the way he did when he talked about computers. "Bad news? You look down in the dumps."

"It's nothing."

"Patrick?"

Never mind, she wanted to say. "No big deal. He has to work tomorrow night, that's all."

Her stepfather looked sympathetic. "That's tough. Can't you do something with your girl friends?"

Honestly! "My girl friends are all cheering. Patrick was going to take me to the game, but he and Tony have to load furniture."

"Tony Pell, the one who dates Hope? Why don't you and Hope surprise the boys after the game with pizza or something? Just show up with it?"

Jessica looked surprised. Her stepfather was making a halfway decent suggestion and laughing. "In high school I worked as a stockboy on the weekends. The girls I went with liked to do crazy things like that, and I loved it. I was always afraid of getting fired, but Patrick doesn't even have to worry about that! Just a suggestion — the cheerleader looks as though she could use some cheering up."

By third period on Friday, Melissa was beginning to think she was obsessed. Before Hope had shown up at Bodyworks had Melissa run into cheerleaders in every corridor? They were everywhere. Jessica in history, Hope in homeroom as usual, Tara walking down a corridor with her for the second day in a row, and Peter waving from the drinking fountain. She caught sight of Sean leaning back against his locker as Diana Tucker held a textbook up to him. She was so blonde and striking and he was so dark and gorgeous, they made a great-looking couple, Melissa thought. However, as she passed them, Sean looked at her and then the ceiling and mouthed, "Help!"

Jessica waved a crutch at Melissa in the library. "Coming to the game tonight?" she whispered.

Melissa shook her head. "I don't think so. I promised my sister I'd take her to the mall."

"Where's your school spirit? You'll miss the big performance, the first without me out there. All new cheers, too."

"Will that make a difference?"

"Will it ever! The squad had to revise every cheer. That's why Coach Engborg wants an alternate, so none of the squad will ever have to work that hard again!"

Melissa held her breath, afraid another invitation to try out was coming, but Jessica was hushed by the librarian and the girls separated. "See you Monday, then," Jessica added.

Olivia went through the lunch line with Melissa again and also asked if she'd be at the game. She, too, admonished Melissa lightly as they reached the register. "School spirit's important! You could watch and see how we do it, too."

At the other end of the lunch line, Diana was listening to Courtney Davidson raving about a dress shop she'd discovered in Deep River. Courtney was on her left, and on her other side two girls she didn't know were talking in the same excited tone, and all of it was driving Diana crazy. Her dieter's breakfast had left her stomach growling before she'd even parked her Volkswagen. Hunger made her irritable and cranky and she had to hold back the desire to tell Courtney that no dress shop could compare with the stores she'd left behind in California.

"It's true," one girl was saying to her friend. "The cheerleaders invited her to a pizza party and asked her to try out next week! Isn't that the most awesome thing you ever heard? My own sister! And even better, Peter Rayman drove her home. Peter Rayman, right in my own driveway! Sean Dubrow came with Hope Chang one afternoon and watched — "

"Diana Tucker, will you please answer me? Do you want to go shopping in Deep River and try out this place or not?" Courtney underscored her irritation with a tug on Diana's sleeve.

"Try out? Of course I'm trying out."

Courtney looked baffled. "What?"

They reached the register and fished out their money as the girls ahead of them moved away to a table. "Who are *they*?" Diana demanded. "The one who was right next to me?"

Courtney scanned the crowded cafeteria before heading for the boys' table in the corner. "How should I know? I'll ask around. Come on, Troy and Doug won't wait forever."

As soon as dinner was over, Melissa took a long shower. With her blow dryer, she bent over and dried the long, chestnut hair and then pulled on a pair of jeans and navy sweat shirt with a bust of Beethoven on it. Since she'd have her parka on while they shopped, she didn't much care what she wore underneath.

She was upside down, again, brushing out her hair when the boom of her bedroom door being slammed made her straighten. Molly was pressed against it, her eyes shut.

"My gosh, what is it, Molly!"

Her sister opened her eyes. "They're downstairs!"

"Who?"

"Sean Dubrow and Peter Rayman, that's who! Right in *our* living room, talking to *our* parents! Oh, Melissa, you're the luckiest girl in the whole world. Sean has a girl with him, but who cares?

He and Peter are in their uniforms, and they're standing right on our rug!" Molly's dreamy expression changed to horror as she looked Melissa up and down. "Missy, you can't go out like that!" Molly turned and rushed back out before Melissa could reply.

"Out? I'm not going out, I'm taking you to the mall," muttered Melissa to herself.

The door slammed open again. Molly reappeared, grinning. "Mom says come down to see your friends. You want me to tell her that you just got out of the shower and you're hurrying?"

"Don't you dare say I was in the shower," Melissa hissed. "Just say I'll be down."

Molly laughed. "Boys take showers, too. Don't be so hopeless. Now get out of those gross clothes." She headed for Melissa's closet.

"There's nothing wrong — "

"Hopeless! You want to make an impression," Molly said, sliding hangers aside. "Which is almost impossible with this stuff. Honestly, you spend so much time with your own reflection at Bodyworks, you probably think this is how everybody dresses." She came out of the closet with the gray pleated pants Melissa had worn to Hope's. "These'll have to do. I'll loan you a top. Missy, you really should pay attention to what everybody wears at school, especially if you're going to be a cheerleader."

"I'm not!" Melissa called after her, but Molly had already run across the hall to her own room. She was back by the time Melissa had pulled on the pants. Molly handed her a yellow top, a silver link belt, and a butterfly hair clip.

When the sweater and belt were on, Melissa pulled her hair back and reached for a band.

"No way," Molly said, yanking it from her. "Keep your hair long, put the clip on the side, and *go downstairs!*"

"I'm only going down to tell them that I'm driving you to the mall."

Molly grinned. "Sure! Get going. Wait, lipstick . . . and hurry up. They're on their way to the game, and they can't wait forever."

As she left her room Melissa said to Molly, "They're not here to take me out, silly. They have to cheer tonight."

Melissa walked slowly down the stairs watching the back of Peter's and Sean's shoulders as they stood in the archway to the living room talking to Mrs. Brezneski. There was a girl between them with wild hair and glasses, and all three turned as Melissa got to the bottom step.

"Melissa, this is Kate Harmon. I was just telling your parents that we came over to see if you'd keep her company at the game tonight," Sean said.

Kate was grinning. "I go to St. Cloud and they're playing Garrison, but Sean has the crazy idea that I'd rather watch him than my own team. I said okay, as long as I can make faces at him and I don't have to sit by myself."

Melissa's palms were already moist. "I don't think I can, I'm sorry."

The moment she opened her mouth, Molly interrupted from behind. She had come into the room in her coat. "Mom, you promised to take me to the mall. I'm all ready!"

Anne Brezneski looked at her younger daughter. "Did I? Then let's get going. The game sounds like a lovely idea, Melissa." She shook hands with Kate, Sean, and Peter and told them she hoped they'd come by again.

Deserted by her own family! Melissa watched as her sister and mother left.

"We're kind of in a hurry," Peter added.

"If you say no, Kate'll go to her own game; I'll be so depressed I'll mess up the cheers; the fans will notice, lose their spirit, and upset the basketball team; and we'll lose. So you see, Melissa, the entire outcome of the game depends on this moment." Sean gave her a triumphant smile.

Melissa looked at Peter. "Why don't you come along with Kate?" he asked. She gave up.

"Okay, I'll get my coat."

CHAPTER

9

The only car in the driveway was Peter's old green Ford. Melissa slid into the passenger seat and half turned under her seat belt to listen to Sean's stories as they headed for the Tarenton High parking lot.

Between Sean's jokes and Kate's retorts, Melissa didn't have to worry about making conversation. "The least you could have done this morning was rescue me, Melissa! There I was at my locker when Diana Tucker started babbling about chemistry problems." Sean raised his voice to a falsetto. "Oh, Sean," he cooed, "I'm so dumb and you know all the elements on that chart. Could you just take a minute to explain them to me?" He batted his eyelashes at Kate. "My only hope was Melissa. I saw her coming, I whispered *help*, but all she did was wave and keep walking."

Melissa laughed. "I thought you were enjoying all the attention. Aren't you being a little hard on

Diana? Maybe she really does need help. If she's going to make the cheerleading spot, she probably wants to be friends with all of you."

Peter swung the car through the entrance and around to the parking area closest to the gym. "She's tried every dirty trick in the book to break up the squad and get herself on. Now she's reversing herself, being sugary sweet to all of us."

"People can change," Melissa said quietly. "She cheers all the time in gym class. I've seen her and she'll win by a mile. I can't believe you ever thought I'd stand a chance against her. She's probably done all that rotten stuff because she's been trying too hard. Once she's on the squad, her whole personality might change."

Sean moaned as they got out of the car. "Trust me, Melissa, the way she is now is just as bad as the way she was before. Diana's idea of nice would freeze water."

As they headed toward the entrance, Peter had to fight the urge to pull Melissa into a hug. A wave of protectiveness swept over him. If Melissa changed her mind about trying out and Diana got wind of it, there was no telling how mean things could get. He glanced at Sean, hoping he shared the feeling. They were playing with fire and the feelings of somebody who might not know enough to fight back.

The gym was sparsely settled with kids finding places in the bleachers. Sean and Peter headed for the locker rooms while Kate and Melissa climbed to the middle of the bleachers. They watched the team warm-ups and made conversation until, after half a dozen attempts to keep Molly's clip in her hair, Melissa finally sighed. "Kate, I'm going to the girls' room to fix my hair. I never wear it down and it's driving me crazy. Save my place?"

"Sure," Kate replied and waved her off.

Melissa combed out her hair and wound it back up as girls trooped in and out through the doors at either end of the bathroom. Finishing, she followed the last girls out, but the voice of a girl coming in the other door stopped her out of sight around the corner.

"I could have Sean Dubrow in a minute if I wanted him," the voice was saying. "You should have seen him today, hanging all over me, trying to convince me to let him tutor me in chemistry. He just melted right at his locker."

"I thought he went with somebody from St. Cloud," a second voice replied.

"Kate the dishrag? Get real, Courtney, does she look like any competition for me?"

"I don't know, Diana, I can't keep up with you and your crushes. Anyway, speaking of competition, Molly Brezneski's the name of the girl who was next to you in the lunch line. You know, the one who was talking about her sister? You wanted me to find out — " still hidden from sight around the corner, Melissa froze.

The sentence was smothered by raucous laughter and choking. "No way! *Molly* Brezneski? That means the squad asked Melissa to try out next week. I can't stand it! So that's what Sean and Peter are up to. This is hilarious. Melissa's a total loser, a mouse. The only time she talks is when she's proving how smart she is in class." Diana began to laugh again. "I cannot possibly believe that anyone on the squad would think she has a chance against me. It's too funny! They must be scared to death, and all they can come up with is pitiful Melissa! A total mouse, Courtney." She was still laughing as they left the bathroom the way they'd come in.

Melissa stood rooted to the tile, her cheeks flaming. Part of her wanted to die on the spot, and she blinked as she fought the hot tears welling up in her eyes. Part of her wanted to die, but part of her was enraged. She looked in the mirror over the sink. A total mouse? Who was Diana Tucker to say such hateful things? Diana had to be dealt with. And Melissa intended to do it.

"You're awfully quiet," Kate said during the first quarter as she pushed her glasses against the bridge of her nose.

Melissa agreed. "I'm just concentrating. I want to watch the squad, see how they move together. They all seem so different from each other, but when they're out there, they're so unified. I never noticed before."

"Sudden interest, huh?" Kate was smiling.

"Maybe." She glanced at Troy Fredericks as he dribbled down the court, and watched Olivia as she shook her pompon and called his name. At the next time-out, the squad hurried into position and brought the fans to their feet with their walkovers and handsprings. They all seemed to be making eye contact with *her*, however, enough so that Diana Tucker turned in her seat to look.

All she saw was Melissa sitting next to Kate,

who was sticking her tongue out and making faces at Sean. "How immature," Diana sneered to Courtney.

The Tarenton Wolves won the game easily, and as the squad ran into formation for their final victory cheer, Melissa looked down at Diana, who was studying the moves like a wolf herself.

Although she had a week to go without putting any undue stress on her foot, Jessica no longer needed the support of the crutches, and after the game she returned them to the team physician. Daniel Bennett not only suggested that his step-daughter surprise Patrick with pizza, he also offered his car, and as soon as Hope finished in the locker room, she and Jessica planned to be off.

As the girls changed and Jessica sat on the bench, Olivia brushed out her hair. "Step one worked like a charm. Peter and Sean got Melissa out there."

"She looked like she was studying us and having a good time. Kate's easy to talk to. That helped," Hope added. "But I'm still worried. The problem might have been the boys, but from the way she looks at them, I think she's got crushes on both of them now!"

"So?" Tara asked.

"So Melissa's a very sensitive person, you know that. As much as I want this to work out for us, I don't want her to get hurt, not by Sean and not by Peter."

Tara made a face. "Just because things didn't work out with you and Peter doesn't mean he's going to walk all over her. Give him some credit.

Besides, she's turned us down about a million times, anyway. Maybe we should try to help Heather instead."

"She's not nearly good enough," Jessica said from the bench.

"Great. Well, why don't we just accept the fact that a week from tomorrow night, we'll be in here changing into our uniforms with Diana."

"Now *there's* somebody Peter can walk all over," Olivia muttered dryly.

Jessica stood up. "Hope, let's get out of here. It's too depressing."

Twenty minutes later, with a large pepperoni and a large double-cheese pizza in boxes and a six-pack of soda, Hope and Jessica drove from the Pizza Palace to meet Patrick and Tony. "I can't stand this," Jessica groaned as the smell of tomato sauce and cheese filled the car. "Even *watching* the cheers builds up an appetite."

"Just think what loading a van does," Hope added.

Jessica frowned. "I thought Patrick said they were doing all the paper work and inventory."

"Maybe I'm wrong, but I thought Tony said they'd be loading."

They reached the mall with ten minutes to spare and drove directly to Tarenton Furniture. The loading area was well lighted and easily reached, designed for shoppers who could pick up their purchases themselves. Hope and Jessica scanned the area. There was a utility truck, a Jeep Wagoneer, and a couple putting a bedside table into the back of a station wagon.

"I'll check," Jessica said, getting out of the car. She walked gingerly to the door, grateful she no longer had to maneuver herself with crutches, but as she stepped inside, the lights flickered. Over the P.A. system, it was announced that the mall was closing. At the order desk, she caught the attention of a harried-looking clerk.

"Can you tell me if Patrick Henley from H&T's TLC Moving Company is working here tonight? He'd be in the warehouse, I think," she said, trying to be pleasant.

With a shrug he pushed through the swinging doors and reappeared as the first row of lights went out. "He and his buddy were here about seven," he said as he came back through the doors. "They're on a delivery of waterbeds to Grove Lake. They won't be back tonight."

The expression on Jessica's face told Hope all she needed to know, and as they left the mall, the only sound in the car was a hiss as Hope cracked a soda and offered it to her fellow cheerleader.

The crowd at Dopey's was jubilant, made up primarily of celebrating Tarenton High students. The jukebox had been fed, and while rock music played, Peter took Melissa's parka and hung it with his. They slid into a booth across from Sean and Kate, with Olivia and David Duffy and Tara in the booth behind them. David, a sports reporter, was the one to announce that St. Cloud had beaten Garrison.

"See?" Sean teased Kate. "They didn't need your spirit tonight. Your team won all by itself."

Kate looked at Melissa. "If Sean had his way,

all I'd do is sit in the bleachers and admire him."

Melissa laughed. Kate Harmon was as easy-going and witty as Sean. Although Melissa was angry and hurt over what Diana had said, it was less painful with Kate sitting next to her.

Once they were settled, Peter caught Sean's signal. He cleared his throat. "So, what did you think of us tonight?"

"You were great, as usual," Melissa replied. "I've been to lots of the games in both seasons."

"Yes, but this was the first time you watched while you thought about becoming one yourself." Peter had turned in his seat so he could watch Melissa's expression. Even though Sean insisted that they give it one last try, Peter was trying not to press. What changed Melissa's expression, however, was the arrival of Courtney and Diana. They paused beside the booth on their way to a table.

"Great job tonight, Sean. If your chemistry's half as good as your handspring, I'll get an A for sure. He's going to tutor me," Diana said, looking at Kate. "Sean knows all the little tricks."

Kate smiled back. "From what I hear, you're the one who knows all the tricks, Diana."

Diana's eyes darkened. Be nice, she reminded herself, at least for the week. "Melissa, I thought I saw you at the game! Where's Jessica? And Hope? You know, I was telling Peter at Jessica's the other night about what a klutz I was once in Santa Barbara." She patted Peter's shoulder. "We all make mistakes once in a while, but not tonight, that's for sure!" With a cheerful good-bye, she and Courtney left for their table.

When she was gone, Kate moved closer to

Sean. "Dubrow, if Diana makes the squad, I may have to come to all the games just to make sure she keeps a safe distance."

Melissa drank some of her Coke through the straw. The carbonated drink burned her throat as she relived the humiliation in the girls' room. She'd die before she'd tell any of them what she'd heard. It might not be enough to want to beat Diana at her own game, but it was a start. When she'd swallowed, she looked at the boys. Was she crazy to throw herself in with this squad? What if they were saying the same things behind her back that Diana had?

Why would Peter Rayman and Sean Dubrow want a total mouse, as Diana had called her, on the squad? She wanted to believe what they'd all told her, that she had enough dance ability to make the transition. What other reason could there be?

Melissa looked shyly across the booth at Sean, and then at Peter. "Do you and the others have some free time this weekend?" Her heart was pumping so frantically, she could hear her pulse in her ears.

"Sure, what's up?" Sean replied.

"I'd like to try out for the squad, but I'll need some help."

Peter looked stunned. "Run that past me again."

This time Melissa blushed. "I said I'd like to try out for alternate cheerleader, but I need coaching — a whole lot of coaching."

Sean let out a whoop that turned heads from one end of Dopey's to the other.

CHAPTER

 10

What had been a booth for four, suddenly held seven as Olivia, Tara, and David scrunched in to hear the news. "Outrageous!" Tara cried, trying to keep her voice down. "Melissa, this is the best news we've had all week."

"Please don't expect miracles. I just said I'd try my best, that's all."

"That's enough! It's all we need," Olivia added.

Melissa sighed and wished she felt as optimistic as the rest. Sean looked over his shoulder. "We might want to keep this down. I don't want Diana snooping around with another one of her spy routines."

"It's too late, she already knows you've asked me."

"How? Are you sure?" Peter asked.

Melissa could remember Diana's words all too clearly, but she only said, "I've heard her, that's how I know. But she doesn't know I said yes, if that's any help."

"It sure is, and let's keep it that way," Peter continued. He looked at each face at the table. "As far as anyone here is concerned, Melissa turned us down. That's the rumor I want circulating."

Sean broke in. "If she's seen with us, we'll play up the romance. Peter and Melissa are an item as of right now, got it?"

There were so many of them jammed into the booth, Peter could feel Melissa tense up. "Do you mind not talking as if we're not here?" Peter muttered.

Sean looked helplessly at Kate. "What did I say?"

Kate shook her head. "Forget it. You meant well, for once. Melissa, you'll have to be a super actress from now on and pretend that you actually like these Neanderthals. Look how well I do it!"

The joke broke the ice and Melissa began to relax again.

"The next question is, where do we practice so nobody finds out?" Olivia asked.

"Bodyworks," Sean replied. "We've got the rest of the weekend, and Diana doesn't know anything about it. It's perfect." He looked startled as Kate jabbed him in the ribs. "Sorry! How do you feel about that, Melissa?"

"Okay, I guess."

"Great. Then next week while we're at practice, Jessica can work with you and maybe a few of us can put in an hour or so," Tara added.

Melissa smiled bravely, but all the while she kept thinking, what have I done?

There was as much tension in the Garrison girls' locker room as if a championship game were about to be played. Lockers slammed, one cheerleader snapped at another, and all three of them were icily silent as Mary Ellen came in from her office. As she pulled on her coat, she broke the silence. "There was nothing wrong with the way you cheered tonight. You all did a great job. Nobody missed a beat. Games can't always be won by the enthusiasm of cheerleaders."

Each of them kept busy with hairbrushes or shoelaces. Martha applied lipstick, Amy snapped in a barrette.

Mary Ellen counted to ten as the last of her patience drained away. "I'm speaking to you, and I expect you to look at me and at least pretend you're interested in what I have to say." She waited with her heart thumping while they raised their heads. "If the Tarenton squad had acted like this before, during, or after a game, Coach Engborg would have them doing laps around the gym until the sun rose."

Martha looked at Amy before she spoke. "But we're not the Tarenton team, and you're making sure of that!"

"May I ask what that's supposed to mean?" Mary Ellen replied.

"It means you're making sure that we do nothing but old cheers, nothing to surprise anybody, or fire up anybody. The team probably thinks we don't care at all!"

Mary Ellen sank onto the bench. "Can't you see that all I wanted you to do was stay with the cheers you knew — Garrison cheers, not mine? I didn't want you to think I'd come marching over here determined to change you into my old squad. That's why I stuck with the old ones. That's why I cut out the ones Rusty said were too tough."

"Well, it backfired," Andrea added. "It was a stupid plan."

Nobody gave an inch and the resulting silence was as sullen as ever. Instinct told Mary Ellen that if she didn't act like the authority figure she was supposed to be, she'd be lost, more lost than she already was. "Sarcasm and back talk are bad enough with your friends. But you don't use it with teachers, and you don't use it with coaches. Five laps, each of you."

"What?"

"Five laps and while you're out there, think about what it takes to make a squad work, where the leadership comes from."

"The gym's dark, and what about the boys?" Amy whined.

Mary Ellen knew better than to back down. She marched them ahead of her right into the darkened gym, and fumbled along the wall for the switch. Before she lost her nerve, she pulled back the boys' locker room door. "Woman in the locker room," she called. "Five laps, pronto!" After they listened to her terse explanation, they got back into sneakers and started the run.

"Pathetic," Amy mumbled.

"An extra one for you," Mary Ellen said, but as she leaned against the wall and watched them jog, she had no feeling of accomplishment. They were no better off than they'd been before.

At ten o'clock that Friday night, the phone rang and Jessica pulled it into her lap. She was on the couch, watching television. "It's about time I heard from you! You and Tony missed pizza and sodas, not to mention my sparkling wit and Hope's sense of humor."

"Tony and me? I was with Duffy eating burgers and fries. Where were you?"

Jessica's heart fell. "Olivia? I thought you were Patrick."

The cheerleading captain laughed. "So I gather. Sorry, your night sounds pretty awful, but I've got some news that'll cheer you up. Melissa said yes! We're starting with her tomorrow at Bodyworks." She gave Jessica all the details, including the plan to keep the news from Diana.

When Jessica finally hung up, the TV news had finished, and she gave up on Patrick, knowing he wouldn't call so late. They seemed like strangers, hardly grabbing more than a few minutes here and there. Without cheerleading practice to fill her afternoons, Jessica's days were dragging. At least coaching Melissa would give her something on which to concentrate.

Melissa was exercising at the barre at Bodyworks, horrified at how damp her palms were. Molly had made her change her leotard twice, insisting that the lavender one looked the best with her navy legwarmers. She added a pink sweat shirt and her hair was in braids, fastened Austrian style around her head, a method required by the Royal Ballet of its younger students. Molly had taken one look at it and groaned, but Melissa kept the braids anyway.

"Tah-dah!"

The male voice startled her and she looked over to the door. Sean and Peter, in jackets and warm-ups, were grinning at her. "Mikhail and Baryshni-kov, at your service," Sean said lifting his foot cleanly to the barre.

Melissa smiled slowly. "I'm not any better at cheering than you are at ballet. And please don't make me begin until some of the girls have arrived," she added silently. Since Sean's pronouncement that she and Peter were to pretend to be a couple, she could barely look at him. After they'd left Dopey's, Peter had dutifully walked her to her front door and talked about how glad he was that she'd changed her mind. But he didn't seem glad; he seemed anxious and worried. It hadn't helped that she'd dreamed all night about pas de deux and promenades with Peter as her partner.

It was a major relief when Tara followed them in, calling, "Mikhail and Baryshnikov — that's a new slapstick comedy team, right?"

Fifteen minutes later, the entire squad was assembled for Melissa, with all but Jessica demonstrating three simple cheers. Besides "Give Me a T," in which Melissa and the other hopefuls would spell out the school's name, Olivia thought they should chose ones with graceful leaps and midair splits. "Instead of the gymnastic moves which the others'll do, I'm sure. They're more spectacular, but these are closer to Melissa's ballet steps. She'll do them perfectly and they'll contrast with Diana's California stuff."

She looked at Melissa. "Heather Mazanec and Andy Taylor, the other two who've been asked to try out, aren't as good as you'll be, I promise. Diana's the real competition. Now let's get cracking."

It was Sean who tugged Melissa by the wrists and got her to stand in front of their single file. Then, as Olivia signaled, they began in unison:

"Move 'em along, with all your might,
We've got the spirit, we've got the fight!
Wolves are gonna score, dribble left,
    dribble right,
Tarenton knows, tonight's the night!"

While she watched, the girls linked arms and kicked, toes pointed, legs straight. Behind them, Sean and Peter did jumping jack variations, and when they reached the last line, they all knelt, pushed pompons forward, and in a fluid motion jumped up into perfect arcs, knees bent, heads to one side, smiles dazzling. Sean and Peter did handsprings forward and everyone ended with their arms open to the imaginary fans.

Jessica and Melissa clapped, but Melissa dropped her hands as they gathered around her. Tara urged her into position, Olivia explained the moves, Hope tried to hand her a pompon.

"Hold it!" Everyone stopped and looked at Peter. This is worse than Hope's pizza party, he thought. She'll never last the morning with this confusion. While he still had their attention, he stepped forward and took Melissa by the hand, tugging her gently into the middle of the room.

"Forget everything you just saw," he said quietly. "What you need are the basics. I don't know much about ballet, but I do know you have to move from the waist, from an axis. Cheerleading's just the opposite. Arch your back, bend your knees. You can't look like a dying swan or a fainting princess anymore. You have to look totally happy and ready to run a marathon even if you're dead on your feet!" He looked at the surprised faces around him. "Olivia and Hope, put Melissa in the middle and do another kick line."

Olivia saluted. "Yes, captain!" Nevertheless, she agreed with what he was trying to accomplish, and as she and Hope put their arms around Melissa's waist, they counted: "One-kick, two-kick, three-kick, four." Melissa raised her own leg, pointed her toe, and fell perfectly into place.

"Move 'em along with all your might," she called as she continued alone, but when she stopped she shook her head. "Don't get too excited, I've been doing these kicks all my life."

"It's a great place to start," Peter replied. He motioned for Sean to step behind her. "Lifts, now. The minute you feel Sean's hands or mine at your waist, that's the signal that we're in position and ready to start. Bend your knees and put your hands over Sean's. That's *your* signal, so we know you're ready." Peter stopped long enough to give Jessica an apologetic look as he remembered how *un*ready they'd been. It was nice not to feel guilty anymore, however, and Jessica looked as though she felt the same way. He turned his attention back to the student. "Bend your knees and push off. There must be something like this in dance."

Not with Sean Dubrow and Peter Rayman, Melissa wanted to reply. She'd never felt so self-conscious in her life, and Sean's hands on her waist weren't helping things one bit. She wasn't a clumsy person, yet over and over she'd land on the side of her foot, or too loudly, or worse, nearly on top of whichever boy was trying to support her.

She smiled when Peter handed her two pom-pons. "Do an arabesque with these," he said, "and remember to shake them."

Sean and Peter stepped back with the others, and watched Melissa's improvisations. Her first was serious, her second, playful, and as the rest of them watched, she shook the pompons during each leap, letting her body bend and arch, bend and arch.

Tara nodded at Peter. He was a genius! With the pompons, strict ballet was impossible and Melissa had an excuse to loosen up. Her silliness actually improved her moves and the less self-conscious she was, the more gracefully she cheered.

CHAPTER

After an hour and a half of carefully chosen moves, Olivia called a break to the Saturday morning tutoring session. Melissa's braids no longer stayed fastened, and she looked exhausted. "Enough for one day," the captain said, patting Melissa's arm. "You're doing great."

"I don't know about that. I'd like to stay for a while and practice by myself, without you guys staring at me. I have a lot to review before we start up tomorrow." She smiled at each of them. "Besides, I have a sneaky feeling things will get much tougher."

"Nothing you can't handle," Sean replied easily. "Maybe I'll stick around and work on my arabesques." He did a series of off-center leaps.

"Daffy Duck, maybe, Mikhail, no way," Tara called as he landed flat-footed at the barre and tried again to lift his toe to the rail.

"How about coming with us for lunch first?"

Tara added to Melissa when they'd stopped laughing.

"Not before I finish. Thanks, anyway. You go ahead. I'll see you tomorrow."

When they were sure Melissa didn't mind, Jessica, Hope, Tara, and Olivia went down the stairs and out to Tara's car. "Boy, does it feel great not to be loading my crutches in here," Jessica said, sliding carefully into the backseat. "Where to?"

"How about the salad and juice bar at Pineland Spa? We have a family membership," Tara replied.

"Sounds better than the cold double-cheese pizza in my refrigerator," Hope replied.

"Not left over from your party?" Tara said.

Hope shook her head. "No, left over from not being able to track down Tony and Patrick last night."

"Don't remind me," Jessica groaned. But before Jessica could begin to mope, Tara backed the car from its parking space and asked the all-important question.

"Do we think Melissa stands a chance?"

"Of course! It's easy to see what a natural athlete she is. Peter was brilliant to think of giving her the pompons while she did the arabesques. The sooner she's comfortable with the bending — "

"And comfortable with the boys," Jessica added.

"And the boys," Olivia repeated, "the more natural she'll be."

"It's good to see Peter so interested, too," Hope

112

replied. "Since we broke up, he hasn't been himself. I'm really glad to see him take an interest."

"There's more to the problem than the cheers, though," Tara said from behind the steering wheel. "Did you see how loose her hair got? She can't cheer with it long, and it'll look awful in dangling braids."

"A little blusher wouldn't hurt, either," Jessica added.

"I don't know. She has beautiful eyes and cheekbones," Hope said.

"All of which are lost at ten feet, the way she looks now," Jessica answered. "Maybe we could talk to her at lunch on Monday."

As usual, Hope remained thoughtful. In the backseat she brushed back her own straight, black hair. "We can't ask her to cut her hair. It's nearly to her waist, and what if she did that for us and then lost the tryouts? I'd ask her to wear iridescent eyeshadow first."

Tara parked the car in the lot. Saturday afternoons the spa was crowded with raquetball players, exercise students, and executives just trying to relax after a hectic week. Jessica followed her friends to the entrance, trying not to think about how nice a Saturday afternoon would have been with Patrick. Work, work, work!

The juice bar was crowded with men and women dressed as the cheerleaders were, in fleecy warm-ups and casual outerwear. Once they'd slung their jackets over the backs of chairs at a circular table, the girls grabbed trays and got into the lunch line.

"Rabbit food," Tara muttered, heaping a salad

together from the bowls of ingredients.

"But good rabbit food," Olivia said.

When the girls had filled their trays, Tara signed her family's name and membership number on the tab at the register. As she pivoted with her tray, she nearly bumped into Diana Tucker and Courtney Davidson, who were taking their place in line.

Diana looked the four of them over. "Practicing cheerleading way out here at the spa?"

"Yes," Tara replied before the others could contradict. "With Jessica out for the week, we need lots of extra time, and it seemed like more fun out here than back in the boring old gym."

Diana arched her eyebrows. "No boys?"

Olivia cleared her throat. "We're just going over the female routines. Sean and Peter weren't needed."

Diana looked dubious. "There's not an empty room in the building, but whatever you're up to, aren't you glad it won't happen again? Coach Engborg finally took my advice about an alternate. Of course, she's holding tryouts just to make it all fair and square. She and I already know the outcome, of course. You'll really love the way I jump, the way they do it in Santa Barbara. I can fill you in on Friday before the Alumni-Varsity Game. That's when you get to introduce me." She gave them a bright smile that would have fooled anybody who didn't know what was going on. Diana began to move to her own table and then stopped. "By the way, I heard you asked Melissa the Mouse to try out."

"Of course," Hope replied immediately. "Coach

114

asked us to drum up some interest, but Melissa turned us down. She's not the right type, anyway. It was Peter's idea, since he's going out with her."

Peter's and *Sean's* idea, Diana thought to herself, recalling the bet she'd overheard.

"Nobody can beat you, Diana, but Coach wanted a few others, as you said, to make it fair. Good luck," Olivia added as she sat down, hoping Diana would miss the fact that she was choking on her words.

When the cheerleaders were alone again, they looked at each other and sighed. "Do you think she believed us?" Jessica said.

"Of course. She's so wrapped up in herself, why wouldn't she? I can almost see the wheels turning. First she'll get on the squad as an alternate, then she'll see to it that one of us is out for every game. Flat tires, stolen uniforms, made-up emergencies. I'll bet she's already thought up a dozen tricks."

"There's no trick, you just throw your head back and arch." As Sean talked, he bent into a jump and landed on his toes, bringing his hands to his waist as if he were Melissa. "Now Peter's behind you. Wait for his hands at your waist, bend, and up! He'll double your height. It's a great effect."

"If I don't fall all over the place," Melissa moaned. The boys hadn't left as she'd expected. Instead, Sean and Peter put her through a series of arched leaps until her self-consciousness drained away, to be replaced by determination.

She stood in position and looked at the reflection in the mirror. She saw a very intense sixteen year-old mouse of a ballerina with two cute boys behind her. They were grinning, making faces at her, and she began to laugh. "If you do that, I can't concentrate," she complained. How would she ever concentrate with the two of them so close?

"Okay, here I go," she blurted. She concentrated on a distant mark, her face a mask of concentration. Melissa knelt, pushed into a jump, and landed lightly on her toes, bent again. Like clockwork, hands gripped her waist, supporting the second leap, and she rose off the floor, head to one side, arms out. "Go, Wolves!"

She came back to earth to the sound of Sean's whistle as Peter let go of her. "Perfect!" Sean cried as Melissa grinned up at Peter's face. Peter pushed her loose hair away from her eyes and her whole face tingled.

"Perfect, and we'll quit while we're ahead," Peter added, suddenly all business. "You can have some peace and quiet until tomorrow." While she stretched her legs, the boys got into their jackets and, after another compliment, left the room as the girls had.

Melissa's heart began to pound furiously, and she hurried to the barre. She felt as though she'd been put into a washing machine on the spin dry cycle. First position, second position, third; she slid her feet and forced the graceful slide of her arm in what was usually a calming set of exercises. It didn't clear her head. Nothing worked. All she saw was Peter Rayman's face in her mind, his sandy hair, his soft eyes, that studied glance.

With a sigh, Melissa slid down against the mirrors in a heap.

She knew they'd only told her she'd been perfect just to build her confidence. How had she ever gotten herself into this mess? If she hadn't let Molly talk her into keeping her hair down and going to the game, she never would have gone to the girls' room. If she hadn't gone to the girls' room, she never would have overheard Diana's mean comments. And if she hadn't overheard Diana, she'd still be a ballerina, happily dancing alone up here in the rehearsal room of Bodyworks, and Peter Rayman wouldn't have to pretend he liked her so Diana wouldn't guess what they were up to. Melissa began to laugh. Boys were enough to drive you crazy — if little sisters didn't do it first.

She got up from the floor and did one routine, a pitiful attempt to be Tara. She was pulling on her navy blue parka when the door opened and Peter came back. "Did I leave my car keys here?"

"Keys?" She followed his glance to the top of the piano.

"Here they are." He lapsed into silence as he took them, and she started for the door.

They reached the door together. Say something, you idiot, Melissa told herself. She and Peter stepped aside as four eight-year-old ballerinas, led by their instructor, entered the room. On the stairs, Peter laughed to himself. "They look like ducklings following their mother."

"Very serious little ducklings. Madame Bourget is very strict."

117

"Did you take lessons from her?"

Melissa nodded as the blast of air reached them on the sidewalk. "For years when I was little." She pulled her jacket closed. "I'm sorry, I always seem to talk about ballet."

"I brought it up," Peter replied. "Listen, there's one of those deejay dances at the gym tonight — would you want to go?"

"You mean so we can be seen together?"

Peter felt a tug in his chest. "Sure, so we can throw people off." He looked from Melissa's face over her shoulder to the gas station across the street. "Speaking of which, Diana Tucker's getting gas and staring right at us!"

Melissa started to turn, but Peter grabbed her arm. "Don't look." He put his arm around Melissa's shoulder and walked her to her car at the curb, wishing she'd do something besides blush and look at her feet. He shouldn't have yelled. He studied her expression and wished he weren't an only child. A few sisters around the apartment would sure help take the mystery out of women!

Mary Ellen finished the practice session of the alumni squad by trying on the uniform the sewing committee had made. She twirled with the others in her box-pleated, knee-length jumper, which would be worn with a white blouse and cable-knit knee socks. As she took the one made for Nancy Goldstein, as well, she remarked, "All we need is some Elvis Presley music."

"The Beach Boys and the Beatles, too," someone added. "Boy, does this bring back memories!"

Mary Ellen waved them all off, happily anticipating the fun of having Nancy back again. The group spanned twenty years with little in common except their love for their school and the cheerleading squad. Nobody was jealous or resentful, nobody had questioned her choice of cheers or her authority. In the week before the Alumni-Varsity Game, Garrison had two of its own scheduled. Mary Ellen was already dreading them.

The cloud of depression began to lift as she neared the turn onto Fable Point. It skirted Narrow Brook Lake, a neighborhood of mansions built when such styles had been fashionable. Their carriage house was a dream come true, the way her love for Pres was. At the sight of his Porsche in their driveway, she smiled, glad to be home. However, there was an unfamiliar station wagon parked next to it and she entered the house wondering with whom she'd have to share his company.

"Here she is," she heard him say in the living room. "Mary Ellen, you have some company."

She hung her jacket on the peg in the kitchen and hurried into the next room. The six Garrison cheerleaders were sitting on the raised hearth. From Rusty to Amy, they all got to their feet as she came toward them.

Andrea Hamel stepped forward. "Coach Tilford, we came to apologize. We've had a major attitude problem ever since you came on as fill-in coach. Last night you were right to let us have it the way you did."

"We've been talking to Pres just now and I feel

119

lousier than ever," Rusty added. "I guess we never thought about how tough it would be for you. We just thought you'd never want us as good as Tarenton."

Mary Ellen tried to smile. Maybe in her heart she didn't, and she was afraid to face the truth. "Tarenton's already perfect. I'd like you that way, too." She went back into the kitchen to get them all some chips and sodas, but as she opened the bag she paused. Is that what I want? Do I really want Garrison as perfect as Tarenton?

"Well?"

"Well what?" Melissa looked at Molly, who had come into her room with an expectant expression on her face.

"Don't play dumb, Missy. What did everybody say when they saw how wonderful you were?"

Melissa laughed. "I wasn't wonderful." She sat down on the bed and pulled off her legwarmers. "Far from it. The only stuff I do right are the leg lifts. I'll never be good enough to win on Thursday."

"Then how was it to have Sean and Peter coaching you, holding you in their arms, pushing you into those leaps?" Molly persisted.

Melissa threw a legwarmer at her. "You watch too many soaps! Sean's in love with Kate Harmon and Peter is just being professional, like a real coach."

"Hopeless," Molly muttered.

"Maybe I am, but who cares? Now if you'll excuse me, I'm going to take a shower and get some lunch. Peter's taking me to the dance at school tonight, and my hair's a wreck from these braids."

She got up and started for the bathroom, but Molly caught up with her in the hall. "He asked you for a date! Another one, two in a row. Holy cow, Melissa, I guess you must be doing something right after all."

"Molly, we have to pretend to like each other so Diana Tucker doesn't know I'm being coached. It's just a plan to make things run smoother. Now keep the secret and let me take my shower!"

CHAPTER

12

Olivia and David Duffy arrived at the Tarenton High gym as Tara finished giving her requests to the disc jockey. The Pep Club sponsored the dances periodically which, unlike the proms and theme nights, were casual, with everybody coming in jeans or comfortable school clothes. Tara chose to come single, the way most of the students did.

"Are Hope and Tony coming?" David asked as Tara approached.

"This music is definitely not Hope's taste. Besides, I think Patrick's got Tony all tied up with some new account. I do know that Kate talked Sean into going to a St. Cloud party. They beat Garrison last night so there'll be a celebration," Olivia answered. She looked thoughtfully at Tara. "I wonder how Mary Ellen felt about losing. A year ago she wouldn't have cared at all who won a Garrison–St. Cloud game. Now she has to throw her whole life into it."

"Well, nobody's forcing her," Tara shot back. "It was her choice and the next thing you know, she'll be making sure Garrison beats us. She didn't have to take the job. If you ask me — "

"Nobody did," Olivia replied in the middle of her sentence. Whatever they felt about Mary Ellen's position wasn't going to change anything.

"Well, speaking of cheerleaders," Tara said, hitting Olivia's arm.

Diana Tucker and Troy Fredericks arrived at the door, paid, and had their hands stamped. Tara thought Diana looked even tanner and blonder than she had that morning. Her face glowed with perfectly applied makeup, and she smiled at Troy as if he were the only boy in the room.

"Mr. Varsity," David murmured to Olivia. "Didn't I do a feature on him during soccer last fall?"

"I wonder how she got him to bring her," Tara said. "Maybe she thinks the basketball team has something to do with the cheerleading judging next week. Wouldn't it be nice to get through one day without worrying about what she had up her sleeve?"

"How about one hour?"

Melissa saw Troy before she saw the others. Just looking at him gave her the same feelings as when Sean teased her or Peter lifted her into an aerial. But when Diana turned and smiled, then snaked her arm through Troy's, Melissa felt as though she'd come down from the aerial flat-footed.

Diana was checking every piece of clothing

Melissa had on and doing nothing to hide her surprise. Melissa smiled wryly. Everything she had on was Molly's, from the red puckered pants and polka dot shirt to the cinch belt. Molly had even done Melissa's hair, which she had repeatedly pronounced to be "about three yards too long," into a complicated wave of French braids and a chignon. Nevertheless, the borrowed outfit was causing a reaction in more than one person — Troy smiled at her as he and Diana passed.

As soon as Peter had paid, they joined the cheerleaders. Tara commented on the belt, Olivia complimented her hair. The loud music made conversation impossible most of the time, and Melissa began to relax.

Peter was glad to see her happy. The more she hung around with them, he thought, the more at home she'd feel. That could only make the cheering better. Melissa was fun to be with and made him feel good. Even if she didn't win on Thursday, it was worth the effort.

He went off to get them both Cokes when a voice behind Melissa made her turn. "So you and Peter are dating, I see," Diana remarked brightly.

"It's no big deal," Melissa replied.

Diana touched her arm. "Don't get defensive. I think it's great. You've obviously come out of your shell. I didn't know you even owned clothes like these. Very becoming. I hear he's tried to talk you into trying out for the squad on Thursday. That's real togetherness."

"I turned him down. I told all of the squad members I wasn't interested." Melissa hated lying, even fibbing made her flustered, and as she blushed she looked beyond Diana to Troy so she could change the subject. "You played a good game last night, Troy."

"Do you think so? I didn't know you were there." Troy looked pleased and surprised, making Melissa wonder if it was her outfit or the fact that she could talk about something besides history and World War II.

"I was with Kate Harmon. She goes with Sean Dubrow."

He nodded. "I didn't know you hung around with them, Melissa."

Peter returned with the drinks and the two boys talked about the game and the Alumni-Varsity Game coming up. Melissa added her opinion on the starting lineup while Diana slouched in boredom against the cement block wall. She watched the three of them, steaming at being so easily ignored.

"Maybe we should flip a coin," Tara said to Olivia from the corner of the gym as they studied the foursome. "Whoever loses has to talk to Melissa about her hair and makeup."

"I thought cheering was the problem," Duffy threw in.

Tara shook her head. "She can't look like that if she's going to make it. Duffy, you know what it takes besides skill. She'll have to sparkle like crazy to outdo the dragon lady. Look at them next to each other over there. Diana looks as though she were born to cheer. Melissa will disappear next to all that blonde hair and blue eyeshadow. Pres is a judge, he'll be looking for the extra quality; and

125

Mr. Stewart sure knows what energy has to come across. But Peter thinks we're pushing her too hard already, so he'll never bring it up."

"How about Hope?" Olivia chewed ice from her cup thoughtfully. "She was great at getting this started. Maybe she's the one to suggest a makeover."

"This isn't bad for day-old pizza," Tony said as he took a slice from the box sitting on the desk in Patrick's office.

Hope pretended to be insulted. "I'll have you know, Jessica and I started all over again. This is fresh — not that you two deserve it."

"Can I help it if I have to earn a living? How was I to know Jessica would chase me all over Tarenton and into the wilderness?" Patrick leaned over and kissed Jessica's cheek.

"It wasn't wilderness, it was the mall. Now I know why the telephone was invented," she replied.

Patrick was still laughing. "I'm glad you used it tonight. If you hadn't phoned, we'd have been gone again. As it is we've got less than a hour."

"Well, you have to eat," Jessica complained. "What a pitiful weekend! All day transforming Melissa from caterpillar to butterfly, and both nights getting indigestion from wolfing down pizza."

"It could be worse. We could be eating in the front seat of the car again," Hope added.

"How are things going with the makeover?" Patrick asked over another slice.

"Great," the girls answered in unison.

"Melissa's got natural ability," Jessica continued. Hope and Tony got into a discussion about the pizza party as Patrick lowered his voice.

"Jessica, Melissa needs your help, and I need your understanding."

Jessica leaned against his shoulder. "Patrick, I understand, it's just hard, that's all. I need you, too."

"Are you still upset about your stepfather playing in the Alumni-Varsity Game?"

"Not upset, exactly. It just feels weird, really weird."

"I promise, even if I lose the furniture account, I'll be there Saturday night for you. You'll be cheering again and introducing the new alternate. It'll be a great night, Jessica."

She sighed. "I hope so."

Hope glanced at the two of them. "Tomorrow's our last chance to give Melissa a full workout. Jessica's our big hope for the week since the rest of us have extra practice. She'll make Melissa a star!"

Patrick kissed Jessica again. "If anybody can work some magic, it's Jessica."

"Thanks for taking me tonight," Melissa said, as she stood with Peter at her front door. She'd worried half the night about this moment. What to say, what to do. . . . What if he kissed her? What if he didn't? What if he did just because he thought he should?

He was looking at her, she could feel it. She no longer thought of Peter as an aloof senior, unapproachable and larger than life. He was becoming a friend. It was easy to be with him, easier and easier.

Melissa closed her eyes for a moment and suddenly Peter's warm mouth pressed against hers. His kiss was soft and she could feel his hands against her hair. When she opened her eyes he was looking at her, smiling.

"You didn't have to do that," she blurted.

He knit his eyebrows. "Didn't you want me to?"

"Yes, well, sure! But I don't want you to feel as though you have to kiss me just because Sean wants us to pretend. . . ." She could feel the heat making her cheeks darken. "You know, Peter. Nobody's around, you don't have to pretend."

"Diana might be cruising by any minute."

Melissa turned her head and looked out at her darkened street while he laughed softly. "I was kidding."

"Oh." She sighed. "I wish I had brothers sometimes. I wish I knew more about how boys think. Sometimes I don't understand any of you at all!"

"And you think girls are easy? Hope and I went together for a long time, but I still get rattled. You're like her in some ways, Melissa. That's probably why she likes you." He smiled at her until she smiled back. "I don't have any sisters, and you don't have any brothers. Maybe we can help each other out."

"You're already doing more than your share."

"I like it, Melissa. The change in you is terrific, even Troy noticed tonight."

"Did he?"

"Aha!"

"Aha, nothing. It's just a little overwhelming

when suddenly in one week, Sean Dubrow, Peter Rayman, and Troy Fredericks all start paying attention to you."

"You're worth paying attention to. Hope was smart about that before we were."

Melissa smiled shyly, warm inside from her tired toes to her tingling face. "You didn't have to say that, Peter."

"I wanted to. I meant it." He kissed her lightly again, and it felt warm, friedly, not pushy or serious, just the way they both wanted it. When she'd said good-night and closed the door, Melissa went upstairs to her room, happy and confident. If ever she could have some brothers, she'd choose Sean and Peter, and if ever there was a group for which she wanted to do her best, it was the squad.

They all noticed it. Melissa moved with determination as if she'd stayed up all night memorizing every cheer she'd seen the squad perform. She had on pink tights and her Beethoven sweat shirt with the sleeves rolled back and now, after the first half hour, she stood at the barre panting with the rest of them — and grinning.

"You've got the round off," Tara said. "You move as though you've been doing this for years!"

"I even dream about it," Melissa replied. "With Mikhail and Baryshnikov on either side of me, how can I go wrong?"

"Now there's a girl with brains," Sean replied, grabbing her wrist and tugging her back onto the floor. "Give us some leaps and then we'll do 'Chugga-chugga.' "

Sean let go and stepped back. Melissa took a deep breath. "I leap, you all stare!"

Peter raised his hand as if to wave away the doubt. "There'll be lots more than just us staring Saturday night."

"But I won't be doing a single!"

"You'll be the one they'll all want to see, though," Tara said. "You'll be the new girl in the spotlight, even with all of us around you."

Melissa seemed lost in thought, and then without another word, she got into position and sprang into a nearly perfect arc. "Go, Wolves!" Before anyone could distract her, she tried it again, closer to the mark. "Go, Wolves!"

"Go, Melissa," they cried as she landed lightly on the tips of her sneakers, one braid breaking loose again from its hairpins. She grabbed it and stuck it back. "I chose this style because the Royal Ballet uses it to keep their hair in place. I never thought cheerleading would make it so tough to keep these things in place."

A look passed among the girls until Hope stepped forward. "You don't want your hair to distract and steal the show."

Melissa stuck in the last hairpin. "Steal the show?"

"Right in the middle of a leap or a cartwheel, one loose braid dangling around your face would make everyone forget how pretty your style is." Hope chose her words carefully and watched for any indication that she'd hurt Melissa's feelings.

"Extra pins for sure, then," Melissa replied. "I'll wind them better, too. Don't worry."

Hope *was* worried; they all were, but things

were moving so well with the cheers themselves that Hope just looked at the others and signaled them to let the subject drop for the moment.

"Chugga-chugga, chugga-chugga, oo, oo!
Tarenton Wolves, we're with you!
We've got the team,
And you've got the steam,
Chugga-chugga, chugga-chugga, oo, oo!"

With Melissa in the middle, the squad fell into formation and marched across the floor, right arm stretched to the shoulder in front, left hand on their own waist. "Awesome," Tara whispered behind Melissa. The glow began again. It was like being in a great big family. As different as they were from each other, as much as they fought among themselves, Melissa could feel the pull and determination of her six new friends. When she overheard Sean whispering, "I think she's got it," to Peter, she thought her heart would burst.

More than anything, she wanted to live up to their expectations. They think I can make it, she kept telling herself. She was determined to prove it.

"Chugga-chugga, chugga-chugga, oo, oo!" They finished with a turn to the mirrors. While Jessica clapped encouragement, they each jumped into a spread eagle and came down clapping.

Olivia caught her breath. "Fantastic. This should be one of your single cheers, Melissa. No one else would think of it because it's supposed to use all of us in a line, but your moves are so effective, I think it would surprise everybody."

131

"I do feel comfortable with it," she agreed.

"Good. Now there's one more thing we need to work on. Eye contact is all you're missing. In the mirror just now, every one of us had our eyes on each other in the reflection."

"And I was looking into the Twilight Zone!"

Olivia smiled. "I'm afraid so. It doesn't matter how good you are, if you don't look ecstatically happy *and* into the crowd, it translates into boredom. Exaggerate, just like on the stage."

Sean stepped next to her. "When the swan dies, even the guys in the last row know 'cause the ballerina goes all limp." While the group watched, Sean went up on his toes, down into a slump, and flapped around among them, trying to look like a dying swan. "Even the ushers know what's going on."

"The ushers would think you ate poison for lunch," Peter remarked.

"My point is, in cheering, it's quick, peppy, and one-on-one. Look 'em in the eye, Ballerina, so they know the cheers are for them. Out on the court, guys like Troy Fredericks will be making baskets like crazy."

Melissa nodded and took it all to heart. They ran through "Give Me a T" again, and then watched as she performed "Chugga-chugga" by herself. She stared, smiled, and moved for the group in front of her until it felt right. And then when it felt right, she did more until it felt perfect. When she stopped to catch her breath, Sean and Peter scooped her up and the girls whooped.

Melissa balanced herself on the boys' shoulders and laughed. "Diana Tucker, eat your heart out!"

132

CHAPTER

13

"Two, four, six, eight, ten, come on Tarenton, meet our friend. . . ." Coach Engborg paused and looked at the squad. "This is where you wait, just a second, while the new alternate runs out, kneels, arms wide. Say his or her name, from the semicircle, and move into 'Chugga-chugga.' "

Monday afternoon practice was well underway and between the cheers for the Alumni-Varsity Game and the introduction of the new member, Ardith Engborg had hours of work for them, hours that would carry the squad right through Wednesday. She clapped and ordered them into formation.

"I want Jessica back here tomorrow. She'll have to watch all of this if she's going to participate Saturday. As far as the tryouts on Thursday, I'd like you to sit up in the bleachers as a squad. I'd like some polite applause for each of the candidates, but nothing more. If your presence makes them nervous, I want to see it. Poise is one of the biggest factors in this. Grin your hearts out at each of them, make them aware of you so I see them at their best. Okay?"

The group nodded obediently, but from Tara right through to Sean, each thought there was one contestant at whom none of them wanted to smile. Ever.

Diana made sure the squad was at practice before she left the building. She'd counted faces, all but Jessica. It hadn't taken more than some sharp observation Saturday night for Diana to figure out that Peter and Melissa were far from passionately in love with each other. Pals, she thought with disgust. They were acting like the best of buddies, not steady dates.

The way Melissa looked at Troy convinced Diana as she put the puzzle pieces together. Melissa with Kate Harmon at a game, Melissa with Peter outside Bodyworks, the rest of the squad in warm-ups at the spa. . . . No, Melissa the Mouse had a crush on Troy, if anybody, but that wasn't what had Diana worried.

Jessica Bennett gave up the school bus when she gave up her crutches. Though Diana had expected to see Patrick pick up the cheerleader, she was sure Jessica left the parking lot in the little blue compact Melissa sometimes drove.

Diana got into her Jetta and headed for town. Pineland Spa was where she expected to find the two of them, but as she approached the block with the gas station and Bodyworks, she slowed down. There was the car!

Diana entered the glass doors cautiously, looking from one practice room into another. The surprise, when it came, hit Diana like cold water. At the top of the stairs on the right, through the glass door, she caught sight of Jessica leaning against the mirrored wall. In front of her a blur of movement transformed into Melissa as she arched and jumped and then executed a perfect cartwheel.

Sharply, Diana sucked in a breath. She stood away from the glass and watched. Not only was the mouse from her history class moving with precision, she was enthusiastic. Jessica applauded and Melissa finished with a beautifully smooth walkover. Melissa Brezneski was better than she had any right to be.

"Garrison, Garrison, we're number one!" The six cheerleaders cartwheeled into their final moves as the crowd rose to applaud the winning team filing into the locker room.

Mary Ellen watched the basketball players go and turned to her group. "You were fabulous!" She patted one, then the other, on the back as they smiled. The spirit had returned, and they couldn't wait until Monday to announce that they'd practiced Saturday afternoon after they'd left the carriage house, as well as Sunday.

Mary Ellen's smile was brave. She wanted them fabulous, didn't she? She followed the girls into the locker room, wishing she felt better.

Things didn't improve at home. After the game she sat with half an ear to the trials and tribulations of Pres's day until he waved his hand under her nose. "Boy, are you out in space, Mary Ellen!"

She blinked. "I'm sorry, I know I am. I've been thinking about the squad. They were great tonight."

"Just what you wanted."

"Too great."

Before she could continue, he sighed and put down the magazine. "I'm trying to be sympathetic, Mary Ellen. You've done so much for me, especially during the accident. When you nearly lose everything, it's hard to take problems like these so seriously, sweetheart. Garrison is all you ever talk about. 'They hate me, they won't work for me, they resent my ideas.' Now they're *too good*! Do you know what you really want? Sometimes I wish you'd never taken the job. I'm sorry if that hurts your feelings, but I've got feelings, too. I'd love for us to talk about something else for once!"

"What was it you wanted to say?" Ardith Engborg stopped in the hall Tuesday morning at the sound of her name. Impatiently she waited for Diana to catch up.

"Well, I wasn't going to bring this up unless I ran into you, but I thought maybe you ought to know that I have reason to believe that the cheering squad is secretly coaching one of the candidates for Thursday's tryouts." Diana waited for the coach to stop dead in her tracks. Instead, she kept her brisk pace down the corridor.

"I don't have a problem with that."

"You don't? It's hardly fair for the rest!" Diana began to trot.

"I wouldn't say that. I'm sure if the squad has chosen to help one of you, it's simply to make sure he or she is good enough to compete. None of the squad will be judging, so there's no conflict of interest. Frankly, I'm glad to know they're taking an interest. In a way, it makes the competition more even. Wouldn't you agree, Diana?"

Who cared about even! The less competition she had, the better she felt. Diana nodded, nonetheless.

The coach patted her arm. "Just do your best Thursday, that's all anyone can ask."

Long after the coach had disappeared through the doors, Diana stood staring. *Her best*? Had that implied that she would win? Did the coach already think she'd be better than the rest? Diana began to relax again. She *was* better, far better. She just needed to remind herself, no matter what she'd seen through the door at Bodyworks.

"So, talk!" Molly Brezneski leaned in her usual spot against her sister's closed door and stared across the room at Melissa, who stood at her mirror, holding her braided hair out over her ears. "There's nothing to say. I'm having a great time. I want the squad to be proud of me. Now give me some time to practice with these. I've got to come up with a way to make them stay put. I'll die if my hair starts to fly around on Thursday."

Molly looked disgusted. "That is definitely not cheerleader hair, Missy."

"I know. Tara drops a million hints, and even Hope's mentioned it a couple of times. I'll come up with something."

"How about coming up with a pair of scissors?"

"No way! It's taken me years to grow it. What if I don't make the squad? Then I wouldn't even have my hair anymore."

Molly shrugged. "You're not going to lose and you don't need your old hair. Let it be part of your old life. Now, how about lipstick and blusher?"

Melissa squinted. "Did they put you up to this?"

"No, but they should have. If Sean or Peter had mentioned it, you'd be at the pharmacy cosmetic counter in a flash. Pretend I'm Peter."

"Fat chance!"

"Well, then, pretend that I know what's good for you."

Melissa hugged her sister. "Sometimes you do, Molly."

Wednesday morning, Diana entered her history class, mentally reviewing the background for the founding of the United Nations. Rumors of a pop quiz had been floating around since homeroom, but she'd been too preoccupied with cheering practice in her rec room to crack a book the night before.

Her concentration turned to disgust as she glanced at the back of Melissa's head. The mouse had pulled her hair into a sophisticated knot at her right ear. She was even wearing makeup! Melissa's cheeks were highlighted with blusher. "Lipstick," Diana murmured to herself and then clamped her mouth shut.

Troy Fredericks turned around in his chair and

said something to Melissa which made them both laugh and Diana frown. An alarm went off in her head. Melissa, no matter how athletic she tried to be, had no sparkle, no personality. The one thought that had kept Diana confident was that Melissa would never look the part. Diana sank into her seat. Things were not going the way she'd planned, not at all.

Hope Chang was struggling over a sheet of math equations when the phone rang in the hall. She heard her mother tell the caller her daughter was not to be disturbed during study hours but in a moment, Caroline Chang was at her daughter's door. "Hope, one of your friends is on the phone insisting it's an emergency call. When I asked the nature of the emergency, she said, 'my hair,' and burst into tears. Perhaps you'd better talk to her."

Hope could hear the sniffling as she put the receiver to her ear. "Hope, it's Melissa. I'm being very silly, I know." Her voice caught and she tried to whisper. "Hope, could you come over? I-I need some moral support. I was going to surprise you, but it's not working out — " A sob made her stop. "Oh, I feel so stupid. I shouldn't have called. Don't tell Sean and Peter."

"Where are you?"

"At Rose Poletti's Beauty Shop. The shop's in her house — "

"I know right where it is. Don't move. Give me ten minutes." Hope hung up, made two more calls to Tara and Jessica, and then ran to her mother. She was still explaining and receiving reluctant permission to go when a car pulled into the driveway. "There's Tara. I'll be back, soon, Mother, I promise!"

Caroline Chang was still shaking her head as her daughter left the house. Olivia and Jessica pulled up to the Polettis' curb right behind Tara, and the four of them entered the basement shop together. Music was playing softly, Rose was at the end of the room with her customer, but all the girls saw was the huddled figure right in front of them in the waiting area with two linen towels draped over her wet head. Melissa's eyes were still brimming with tears. "You brought everybody?"

Hope just smiled. "Girls only. A decision this big needs all the support you can get."

Melissa pulled the towels off. "I got as far as the shampoo and chickened out." She held wet strands in her fingers. "This hair and I have been together for a long time. What if I look terrible? What if I don't make it tomorrow?"

Hope stepped closer. "It has to be your decision. That's why none of us pushed you, Melissa. It's not like putting on lipstick." Suddenly Melissa grinned. "Let's go for it!"

"Why, Olivia Evans, is that you over there?" Rose called from her chair. "My goodness, I've got nothing but cheerleaders tonight. Look who else is here!" She picked up the blow dryer and turned the chair. It was Mary Ellen.

The girls looked at each other. "Hello, Mary Ellen," Olivia said. "Or, Coach Tilford, I should say."

"I've been hearing about the squad," Rose said.

140

Olivia nodded. "Duffy covered your last game. I hear the squad is terrific."

"Nice of him to say so," Mary Ellen replied.

"He just reports what he sees."

"Olivia — "

Olivia put her hand up. "Why shouldn't you be good? You were the best at your old school." The sarcasm stung and Mary Ellen asked Rose to begin drying her hair. Moments earlier she'd been full of curiosity about the girl with the braids. Now all Mary Ellen wanted to do was go home and bury her head in a pillow at the carriage house.

CHAPTER

Diana could have danced down the corridors. Melissa was absent, she was almost positive. Diana hadn't seen her changing classes and as the morning progressed, Diana conjured up visions of broken legs, chicken pox, and stage fright. Any — or all — would do. With Heather and Andy as her only competition, she was back on top.

Even the prospect of an F on the returning history quiz didn't dampen her spirits. Her tan was perfect, her brand-new tights and leotard were already in her locker. She'd spent a fortune on a red and white ensemble to match Tarenton's colors, right down to red shoelaces for her sneakers. Three o'clock couldn't arrive soon enough. Diana was sure she would dazzle the judges and squad alike.

Diana entered history with Troy. "Hi," she murmured, but he was looking beyond her, amazement in his eyes and a whistle under his breath. Diana followed his gaze. Jessica Bennett no longer had her crutches, but other than that. . . . Diana's heart jumped. Jessica turned and caught Diana's expression, and she would have given a month's allowance for a picture of the California girl's face as Diana sank into her seat.

Behind Troy, in her usual spot, Melissa blushed at the attention she was getting. It only heightened her complexion. In the girls' room, Jessica had helped with the blusher. Mascara and lipstick were no problem. The light touch and the pink sweater set off the most perfect haircut Rose Poletti had ever given.

Rose had first braided Melissa's hair and cut the braids off for keepsakes. She left the rest shoulder length, which Hope and Tara agreed was fine.

"Keep going!" Melissa had finally begun to laugh and she'd squeezed her eyes shut while the rest of the squad had looked at one another.

Rose had followed orders and snipped, combed, feathered, and fussed. Then, as the rest of them had stood back, she'd used the blow drier to coax Melissa's dark brown hair into soft waves that fell gently around her face.

"I hardly recognize you," Tara had gasped. "You look total, Melissa, I mean it!"

"Now, for the real test!" Rose had swept off the drape. "Give us a cheer."

Melissa had moved into the middle of the basement room and did a modified version of "Give Me a T." Her hair moved around her face and fell back perfectly with every motion. She'd finished

143

to applause and cheers. The junior's brown eyes had filled again, but this time it was from happiness.

Thursday was a blur of happiness. Sean threw himself back against his locker in exaggerated delight when he saw Melissa's new look. Peter told her she looked pretty. Between classes Melissa mentally rehearsed a million times and her stomach swarmed with butterflies. One or another of the squad was always with her, on the way to class, in the hall, at lunch. When the final bell sounded she hurried to her locker. This is it, she thought, I'm as ready as I'll ever be.

The gym seemed an endless walk away and when she caught sight of Nick Stewart up ahead of her, all the butterflies melted into a lump behind her ribs. Her hands were icy and damp as she clutched her bookbag. Everyone was counting on her; she couldn't let them down.

Intellectual Hope, flamboyant Tara, confident Jessica, calm Olivia; they were all friends now, counting on *her*. Sean and Peter, the closest she'd ever come to having big brothers, had knocked themselves out to keep her laughing. She wanted to hug all six of them, but more than that, she wanted to win for them.

Melissa pushed her way through the swinging doors, into the gym. Behind her, the squeak of sneakers made her turn.

"Well, I guess we're headed in the same direction," Diana said brightly as she caught up. "They even talked you into cutting off that beautiful hair. Boy, I thought I was selfish. I never thought the squad would go that far."

"It was my decision."

"Come on, a ballerina with short hair? I know what they've been up to, Melissa. They've been working on you, one person at a time, for days. I'll bet they just dropped a zillion hints until you *thought* the haircut was your idea, then they all hugged you and jumped around as if you were positively brilliant to think of it. You'd never get me to make a sacrifice that big just for somebody's dumb bet."

Melissa tried to keep her brisk pace, but her footsteps faltered. "This isn't a bet, Diana. The squad asked me to try out and I agreed."

Diana tossed her head and began to laugh, and her golden hair billowed around her face. "Poor Melissa! You've been had, as they say. I thought you'd figure it out sooner than this. Trust me, I've pulled some dirty tricks myself. I know Sean Dubrow and Peter Rayman's type."

Diana waved her hand at Melissa, sweeping over her haircut and makeup, down to the sweater and skirt. "Sean bet Peter that you could be talked into trying out this afternoon. You know, caterpillar into butterfly? It's a bet, Melissa. Sean bet Peter a double deluxe at Dopey's he could work some magic and make you over. Mouse into cheerleader. The funny part is that obviously, once they talked you into it, the bet went even further. It wasn't just Sean and Peter — the whole squad got in on it. So it's the squad against you."

Melissa touched her hair and tried to keep her

breathing even. Confusion surged through her. "You don't know them the way I do. You're wrong."

"Know them! Until last week, how many cheerleaders had ever spoken to you? How many even knew you were alive? Melissa, everybody on the squad knows I'll get the position. Haven't you seen me trying to be nice to them? They've never liked me, but I thought that since I have to cheer with them, I'd at least try to make them change their minds about me. Maybe now you'll see how mean they can be. All of a sudden you've got six new friends. A little strange, wouldn't you say?"

Melissa took a deep breath and looked Diana in the eye. "I heard everything you said about me in the girls' room the night of the St. Cloud game."

Diana put on her best sympathetic expression. "Did you? I'm sorry. I was so hurt from trying to be nice and getting nowhere. . . . I probably said all kinds of mean things because I felt so awful. I didn't mean to hurt your feelings." She looked at her Rolex watch. "I don't care if you try out or not, but you'll sure be doing them a favor if you do. Ask Sean if you don't believe me. I heard them, Melissa. The whole thing's a bet. Ask Sean."

The look of triumph in Diana's eyes made Melissa ache with humiliation and doubt. As the two girls reached the locker rooms, the cheerleaders were standing together outside the gym entrance. "Sean's right down there. Ask him. See you later!" Diana smiled again and disappeared into the changing area.

It was impossible to push the words away. *A*

bet. Melissa touched her hair again. How dumb could she be? She'd never liked Diana, but what she was beginning to feel for the cheerleaders was worse. How they must have laughed at her! In a daze, she walked toward them, looking at their smiles, six suddenly smug-looking smiles. Humiliation moved in waves through her, humiliation and anger and the worst sadness she'd ever known.

"Good luck, we're with you," Hope said, but her smile faded at the expression on Melissa's face.

"Sean, could I speak to you for a minute?" Melissa heard herself say.

He flashed that handsome grin and followed her.

"You'll be super, ballerina, just think about — "

"Knock it off," she growled.

He blinked. "Nerves?"

"Nerves! You're the one with nerves. I know all about what you six are up to. I guess I don't know any of you the way I thought I did. I trusted you, that's what hurts so much. Why, Sean? Did you pick out the plainest girl just to make it a real challenge? Boy, am I stupid! All week I kept hearing how terrible Diana was, how she kept making up to you, being nice to you just to get what she wanted. All the while you were doing the same thing to me! The very same thing, just to win a bet! Well, you almost did win, Sean, but not quite."

"Melissa, I don't understand." Then, for once, he was silent, afraid of what he was hearing.

"Don't make me laugh! Just answer one question, *yes* or *no*. Did you bet Peter that you could make me over and convince me to try out this afternoon? Did you bet a burger at Dopey's?"

Sean didn't answer at first. He glanced helplessly at the others and leaned back against the wall. "Diana. All day today we've tried to keep you away from her. I knew she'd try something at the last minute. Melissa, can't you see what she's doing?"

"I don't like her any better than I like you. You all deserve each other, but at least she told me the truth. *Yes* or *no*?"

"Yes," Sean almost whispered, "but it's not the way you think."

Tears seeped through Melissa's lashes and the back of her throat burned. "I even cut off my hair."

"Squad, we need you in the gym," Coach Engborg interrupted from the doors.

One of them said they'd be right there. "Go on in," Sean ordered. Peter refused and after some quick whispering, he joined Sean. Olivia led the others away.

"Melissa, it was a bet, but it was said in fun because we wanted to get to know you. We thought you had a chance." Peter's soothing voice made her throat worse, and the tears spilled down her cheeks. Seeing them, Sean looked as though he'd been slapped.

"All this time you've been laughing at me."

"No!" Peter put his hands on her shoulders. "No way, Melissa. All this time we've been knocking ourselves out for you. That's true, too. The more we got to know you, the more we saw your

148

specialness. I don't care if you grow your hair to your ankles, you're a natural athlete."

With his thumb, Sean wiped the tears from Melissa's cheeks. "I have no right to ask, but please, Melissa, do something for yourself. Go out on that floor and beat Diana Tucker. She's the only person mean enough to have done this. I did bet Peter, but I had seen you dance. I made the bet because I knew you were good enough, I knew what was inside Melissa Brezneski. Hope knew you were something special and we agreed."

Melissa brushed his hand away and shook off Peter. "How can you expect me to believe this?"

"Because it's true. It's not your haircut or your lipstick, ballerina, it's you," Sean said.

"If you go out on that floor and cheer because you think it's what we want, you'll never win. But if it's what you want, all that specialness will show, just the way it does in that little practice room at Bodyworks. We'd be the luckiest squad in the league if you decided to cheer with us, but it has to be your decision." Peter finished with a sigh and a doubtful look at Sean.

"We've got to go in," Sean added. "Diana Tucker wants you to quit right now and the cheerleaders want you to try out. I think it's time Melissa Brezneski does what she wants." He smiled at her, but the look she gave him felt like a knife in his ribs.

From midway up the bleachers, the six squad members watched without enthusiasm as Heather Mazanec, Andy Taylor, and Diana Tucker shook hands with Pres, Nick Stewart, and Coach Eng-

149

borg. Sean sat through Tara's tirade as she berated him in a harsh whisper for doing anything as stupid as make a bet. On the other side of him, Hope put her face in her hands. If Melissa didn't try out, it would tear the squad apart all over again. She could just imagine the blaming, name-calling, and anger that were bound to erupt. It would ruin what was left of the season.

"Perfect, just perfect," Jessica muttered. Now every aspect of her life was miserable.

From the first bench, Coach Engborg pivoted and looked up. "Quiet up there, please. We want to get started."

The three hopefuls had lined up to begin the group cheer when the locker room door opened. Melissa hurried over to the judges and quickly shook their hands.

From above them, Jessica could hear her apologize and then as the six looked down, Melissa looked up. Her expression was guarded, hurt still lingered, but her makeup was fresh. There was no trace of the tears. Peter's chest tightened. Prove it to yourself, he said silently.

It was over in half an hour. The four of them had done "Give Me a T" perfectly. Diana's clear voice and animation shone. Andy and Heather were good, but trying too hard. Melissa fell somewhere about the middle, Sean thought.

The sophomores did their two cheers apiece quickly, hopefully, and then sat down. Melissa announced "Chugga-Chugga," and Tara caught the look of surprise on the faces of Pres and Coach. Nevertheless, Melissa bounced into the group cheer alone. With one arm extended as if someone were in front of her, she chugged across the floor, her free hand on her hip. Her dark hair moved perfectly as she tilted her head; her voice carried clearly across the gym. Sean blinked. Melissa was grinning as she moved. Smiling, almost laughing at the judges. And then looking quickly up at the squad, Melissa glowed.

Olivia elbowed Hope but then clutched her arm. Melissa's timing was a fraction off, enough to break her balance. Too late to stop herself, she threw her body into the final flip, her arms extended on either side of her. Automatically, her fingers formed the graceful pose of the dance, her wrists tightened, saving her balance. She landed on her sneakered toes one measure off, but perfectly.

Sean gasped softly but as he looked down, Melissa made eye contact with each judge, still smiling as if she'd been flawless. Before she lost her nerve, she bounced back into position and announced her last cheer. She began with a round-off and ended on one knee. This time it *was* perfect.

Diana took her place and smiled, too. Her aloof expression stayed in place as she introduced "Meet the Team." As the squad watched, Diana did a Santa Barbara cheer, incorporating the Tarenton players. "Troy, Troy, he's our man, if he can't do it, Jason can. . . ." One after the other, she introduced the starting lineup. It ended with a cartwheel toward the judges, her aloof, confident expression still in place.

"She was perfect," Tara whispered. "I wish she'd fallen on her nose."

Coach thanked each of the four and then left with Pres and Nick for her office. While they were out, the hopefuls talked among themselves. Olivia could see Diana whispering to Melissa, but from a distance there was no way to guess what was being said. Peter caught Melissa's glance, then Diana looked up at the group as well. Neither girl looked happy. The judges came out and motioned for the group to assemble.

"Andy and Heather," the Coach began, "we all want you to know how much potential each of you possesses. Your efforts were good today, very good. If you could continue with gymnastics and polish your styles, I'd like to see both of you again at the spring tryouts. I'm sorry we couldn't pick either of you today, but thanks very much for trying."

Olivia's heart began to race as Nick and Pres shook hands with the sophomores and offered their own encouragement. Coach cleared her throat. "Now, Diana and Melissa, this part of the decision wasn't nearly as easy to make. You both have the polish and the skill. Diana, your moves would translate nicely to our squad."

Jessica grabbed Sean's hand, as icy as hers. "Nice on our squad," he hissed to her.

Peter's heart sank as Diana smiled. "There's so much I can add," she said sweetly.

Coach smiled back. "And I hope you get the chance. You have another year here, and like Andy and Heather, another chance to try out. But Pres, Nick, and I agree, for now, the alternate position should go to Melissa."

Jessica clamped her hand over her mouth to

keep from cheering while Diana's tan turned scarlet. Comprehension changed Diana's features from aloof delight to fury. "I was perfect. I didn't miss a step! I know every single name of every single stupid boy on the team. *She* nearly fell on her face. I can't believe this. It's totally pathetic."

"Diana, please." Nick Stewart tried to rest his hand on her arm, but she shook him off.

"*They* did this," she cried, pointing up into the bleachers at the squad.

Pres didn't even turn around. "No. They had nothing to do with it. I was on the squad, Diana, I know what it takes to make cheers work. You were technically perfect, but there was more life — more caring — in Melissa. And more style."

"Teamwork's what we're looking for," Nick added. "Melissa's expressions and enthusiasm translated into spirit, a team spirit. We just didn't see the same attitude in yours. Every ounce of energy in Melissa's routines told us she wanted to win, in a way that would carry right up to the top of the bleachers."

"But she blew it! She messed up!"

"Diana, you're making this more difficult than it has to be. Melissa's flaw was more than compensated for by her quick thinking and ingenious moves. She did some instant choreography, very much like the discipline one sees in a dancer. Under very tense circumstances, she was quick, graceful, and composed. If you can come up with that combination in the spring, there'll be a place for you, too. For now, we've decided the alternate position goes to Melissa." Ardith Engborg looked back up at the squad and then to her newest member. "Congratulations, Melissa. And I'll expect all of you here for practice tomorrow."

Diana turned on her heel and stomped to the locker room. Without one look at the squad, Melissa followed her. Heather and Andy lingered to talk with the cheerleaders and judges. As soon as she could break away, Hope hurried to the girls' locker room.

"Cinderella already left," Diana sneered from the bench. "She grabbed her stuff and tore out of here like it was midnight and she'd changed back into a pumpkin."

Hope couldn't stop herself, even though she knew she was about to make an enemy for life.

"There's not a chance of that, Diana. Just like there's not a chance *you* could ever change. And what you are doesn't belong on *any* team."

Diana's mouth dropped open in shock as Hope Chang turned and walked out.

CHAPTER

15

"Who's the team that's number one? Let us hear it!"

Mary Ellen sat on the bleachers and watched her squad as each member cupped his or her ear to the crowd behind her.

"Garr–i–son!" The fans yelled back, filling the high school gym with their cheers.

Rusty nodded his head in a signal and the six of them swung back into perfect cartwheels as the demonstration ended. With pompons shaking, the cheerleaders trotted back to their places, smiling broadly.

Mary Ellen smiled, too and held in the upside-down feeling. The squad was the best she'd ever seen it. It was hard to believe. Mary Ellen blinked as though she could change her focus and they'd suddenly be dressed in the familiar red and white of Tarenton High. Nothing felt right except their skill. A light tap on her shoulder broke Mary

Ellen's daze, and she turned around as the teams went back in for the second half. "Nancy!"

Nancy Goldstein and Pres squeezed their way into the second row and made room for Mary Ellen as she moved up. "I hate keeping things from you, sweetheart, but when Nancy called me at work yesterday and said she could get in a day early, I thought you needed the surprise," Pres explained.

Mary Ellen lowered her voice. "I've never been so glad to see another Tarenton cheerleader in my life! Boy, do I need you."

"That bad? Pres told me all about your problem. Maybe we can talk about it after the game."

"You mean you're not going to spend every spare minute with the math teacher?" Mary Ellen teased.

Nancy laughed and held up three fingers. "My long weekend is equally divided. Time with Mary Ellen and Pres, the Alumni-Varsity Game, and Nick Stewart. Just in case the final third gets out of proportion, though, Pres invited me to stay in your guestroom instead of my house. My folks agree, as long as I stop by for a while."

Mary Ellen hugged them both. "Then we'll have lots of time to talk. I should go back to my seat, for now."

Nancy lowered her voice even more and moved close to Mary Ellen's ear. "Pres and I talked about your situation all the way over here, Mary Ellen. You've always known inside what was right for you. Remember Patrick? Remember falling in love with Pres? They're both special to you, but one's friendship and one's the real thing. Maybe Garrison's like Patrick, Mary Ellen. Maybe this has been your chance to realize that you love cheering and you'll make a great coach, but maybe Garrison's just not the right place for you. These guys are terrific, but if that makes you feel guilty and it makes the squad — this one and Tarenton's — uncomfortable, then it's not where you belong."

Mary Ellen nodded and smiled at her friend before she hurried down to her regular seat. Leave it to Nancy to compare cheerleading teams to boyfriends, but she was right. Nancy had summed up Mary Ellen's feeling perfectly.

Garrison won by twelve points, and as the cheerleaders filed into the locker rooms, Mary Ellen told Pres and Nancy she'd meet them back at the carriage house. She got the basketball coach to find Rusty, Eric, and David, and send them to her office while she gathered up Amy, Martha, and Andrea. When they were all assembled, still in uniform, Mary Ellen cleared her throat. She was surprised to find herself close to tears as she looked from one to the other.

"Coach Tilford, are you okay?" Martha asked.

Mary Ellen looked at them. "Yes, better than I've been in a while, but what I have to say isn't easy. You're a terrific squad." She laughed softly. "I never thought we'd get to this point, but you're so good it's a problem for you and for me."

The six of them looked uncomfortable as they acknowledged the truth. "You're quitting, aren't you?" Eric said.

Mary Ellen shook her head. "No, I'm not a

quitter. But this was a temporary offer, and when my time's up, I'll leave Garrison. I'm not going to extend my contract. I will, however, make sure that whoever replaces me as coach is somebody all of you can work with, somebody who'll make sure you do your best."

Mary Ellen, Pres, and Nancy sat up till after midnight. Nancy talked about college, Pres about the new Tarenton alternate, Melissa Brezneski. Mary Ellen talked about the Alumni-Varsity Game, and for the first time in days, she went to bed happy, as if the weight of the world had been lifted off her shoulders.

Hope's fears had come true. Even though Melissa had won, the squad was quarreling bitterly over Sean's bet. The more he tried to explain the way in which he'd said it, the less anyone supported him. He blamed Hope for starting everything; she blamed him. Tara threw in the fact that they could have done the same work with Heather and had an easier time all the way around. "Heather wanted to try out in the first place, and maybe with our help, she would have won."

"Maybe, maybe, maybe," Jessica muttered. "What good does all this do? The damage is done. Melissa's furious, Diana'll probably burn all our houses down, and I, for one, couldn't care less about cheering Saturday night."

They managed to agree on two things. Melissa needed time to hear their apologies and understand, and she didn't need six of them trying all at once. Hope sighed. "I'll call her tonight. This was all my idea. I'll see what I can do."

"She has to face us at practice tomorrow. We can smooth things over then," Olivia added as they separated in the parking lot.

Peter glared at Sean. "If she cries again tomorrow, Dubrow — "

Sean shook his head. "I feel just as rotten as you do. You know, it's funny. . . . Diana thinks she lost this afternoon, but in a lot of ways, I guess she won."

After dinner, Melissa went to her room. Her mother had wrapped her braids in tissue paper and found a small box for them. Melissa wrote the date on the lid and put them in the cedar trunk with her hand-knit baby sweaters and other childhood mementos. She was closing the closet door when Molly came in.

"It's a good thing you have me for a social secretary, Missy. I know you're not taking any calls and I know you're in a rotten mood, but I thought you might want to know that Troy Fredericks just called. He wanted to know if you'd like to go to the Alumni-Varsity Game while he plays, and then out for pizza."

Melissa turned her head. "Troy?"

Molly grinned. "I told him you'd be cheering. He nearly dropped the phone."

"He must not know about the bet," Melissa muttered.

Molly put her hands on her hips in disgust. "Can you imagine, Melissa? He must think you're cute, or that you're funny, or that you have a great personality. Maybe he thinks you two have some things in common." She dragged her sister to the closet mirror and stared at their reflections. "He didn't know that six friends who really care about you helped *you* bring all that stuff to the surface. You're a swan, Missy, you've always been a swan, and if the cheerleaders got rid of the ugly duckling on a bet, good for them! It's the best thing that ever happened to you." Molly finished in a huff. "Hope Chang's called twice. Her message is to stop acting like a total nerd and cheer up!"

Melissa turned from the mirror as Molly started to leave the room. "Hope said that?"

Molly shrugged. "No, she's too polite. But I could hear her thinking it."

Hope gave up after the second call, although she managed to have a heart-to-heart with Molly. Friday morning in homeroom, she and Melissa exchanged glances but there were lengthy announcements about the Alumni-Varsity Game and auditions for a drama club play and neither of them spoke.

In history Jessica went out of her way to say hello and Melissa barely smiled before turning to talk with Troy. Diana sat with a triumphant expression as if she realized how successful she'd been. Melissa might have made cheerleader, but at least she wasn't happy about it, and that would disrupt the team.

Sean ran into Melissa in the hall, but the way she looked at him felt so painful to him, he kept right on going with barely more than a wave.

Olivia had the most to worry about. As captain,

she wanted the unity that made her job easier, but as they filtered onto the gym floor Friday afternoon, she and the five others were no more unified than they'd been their first week of practice last summer out at the cabin.

Through the glass of the coach's office window, they watched Melissa take her uniform. She tried on the sweater, which was a perfect fit, and turned around for Ardith Engborg. Coach Engborg was pointing to Melissa's hair and the two of them were smiling — the first smiles any of the squad had seen on Melissa all day.

She was still smiling when she came onto the floor. "Let's get cracking," the coach said, ordering them into a "Chugga-chugga."

"She's not only an athlete, she's an actress," Tara whispered to Sean halfway through the practice. Melissa was the grinning, peppy cheerleader they'd all seen at Bodyworks. She took her cues perfectly, executing high jumps whenever Sean or Peter lifted her. Over and over Coach Engborg complimented her until the squad picked up the spirit. Except for the fact that Melissa didn't add to the joking or conversation, there wasn't a hint that she was anything but thrilled to be practicing with the six of them.

At four-thirty, the coach blew her whistle. "You're as good as you'll ever be. I'll see you all tomorrow night. We'll introduce Melissa first thing and then enjoy ourselves. It should be quite a night. Melissa, you have your uniform; Jessica, it's good to have you back. I've got to run. Leave the light on; the custodian'll lock up."

For a moment the seven of them stood outside

161

the locker room doors. "I'm glad to see you're feeling better," Hope offered. "I tried to call you last night —"

"You were terrific just now," Olivia added. "We spent so much time at Bodyworks, I feel like you've been on the squad for weeks."

"Your performance just now deserved an Academy Award," Tara said. Half of them gasped but she shook her head. "No, I meant it as a compliment. Obviously, Melissa, you don't want to have anything to do with us, but you put your own feelings aside. That's the sign of a real pro. The show must go on, as they say."

"My feelings would only get in the way," Melissa said. Her voice cracked and she bit her lip. All day she'd been walking on eggs, and practice had been torture. She felt as though her composure was about to shatter.

She'd put so much effort into not ruining the session, there was nothing left. She glanced at their faces and by the time she got to Peter's, his face blurred. Quickly she looked up at the backboard, willing the tears away, but it was too late.

"Don't, Melissa," Sean said. "Please don't cry. Enough tears."

She put her hand up, but Peter stepped forward, pulling her into a hug. With her face in her hands, she leaned into Peter's shoulder and sobbed until she was calm enough to talk. "This is awful," she mumbled into his shirt.

"I don't know, it feels pretty good to me," Peter quipped, relieved to see the beginning of a smile.

Melissa stepped back and tried to wipe her eyes. "I never wanted this and then I wanted it so

162

much I was afraid to hope. I was afraid to let you all down. You put so much time and energy into me, I wanted to do anything to make you proud of me." She sniffed and looked at Hope, who had tears in her own eyes. "That's why when Diana told me about the bet, I couldn't bare to think it had all been a joke. I was so confused and so angry, I did just what Sean told me to do." She looked at him and sniffed again, this time smiling. "I was so furious with you that I just went out there and won for myself, just to prove I could do it. But that was the easy part. I realized that now I had to be with you, cheer with you guys, who might still be laughing, or at least think I was a total jerk."

Sean sighed. "Nobody's laughing. We were the jerks, Melissa. Diana only told you what she heard, but it was all out of context. What I said yesterday was true. I bet Peter you'd make it because you're so talented. I bet on a sure thing."

Hope wiped her own eyes. "Maybe we were desperate to find somebody better than Diana, but we're all just as excited for you as we are for ourselves."

"I believe you," Melissa whispered. "I'm sorry. I'd like to start all over."

Peter put his arm around her shoulders and Olivia slid her arm around her waist. "The place to start is right on this gym floor tomorrow night."

Jessica took a shower in the locker room, wishing she felt as good about herself as Melissa did. Ten days off the squad made her muscles feel as though it had been ten months. She ached under

163

the stream of hot water, inside and out. Daniel and her mother were going out, and the prospect of going home to an empty house made her take more time than usual to lather her hair.

"Patrick may be working tonight, but that's no excuse to stall," Tara called from the lockers. "Hustle, we don't want to leave you here by yourself."

"Okay, okay," Jessica yelled back. Olivia was going to the movies with Duffy, Kate, and Sean. Hope had plans for a symphony with her parents. Peter had talked Tara and Melissa into checking out a local high school hangout. And I'll spend one more night in front of the tube, turning into a couch potato, Jessica thought.

She hurried through her routine, blow drying her hair and listening to the cheerleaders laughing about the Alumni-Varsity Game. They couldn't wait to get out onto the floor and dazzle everyone. Jessica was as anxious as they were to show off Melissa, but that's where her excitement stopped. The coach had given each of them a name of a starting "old-timer." Hope had Daniel Bennett and when they'd practiced, "Rock and Roll, the blues or punk, Daniel knows just how to dunk," Jessica had nearly lost control. It sounded stupid; the whole idea was stupid! Wasn't it?

CHAPTER

The front porch light of the Bennett house was on, but the driveway was empty, as Jessica knew it would be. Jessica parked her mother's car, grabbed her books, and wondered why she'd bothered to wash her hair.

She fumbled with her key in the back door before she realized it was open. Nervous tension made her stop with her hand on the knob as it was drawn open and there, grinning at her, with an apron around his waist, was Patrick.

"Welcome to Henley's Gourmet Night. It's about time you showed up. Honestly, sometimes I think all you care about is cheerleading."

"Patrick!" Jessica's eyes widened. "Is that my mother's apron?"

Patrick let her in and closed the door. "Sure is. Her apron, her spoon, her kitchen. But they're my ingredients."

"Patrick." Jessica sighed. "I don't understand."

He kissed her forehead. "What's to understand? Man does not live by furniture-moving alone. I thought you and I deserved something more than ginger ale and cold pizza. Hope you like stir-fried Chinese noodles with sweet and sour chicken. It's about all we have time for."

She got out of her jacket and put her books on the counter. "Eat and run back to your work again? Do my parents know you've kidnapped the kitchen?"

"Sure. I made a detour to Marnie's this morning, found your mom, and told her my plan." He pointed his spoon in the direction of the dining room.

Jessica walked past him and snapped on the lamp. The table was set for two, with good china and linen napkins. One place held a single red rose and what looked like two tickets.

"Take a look. I have to stir the pea pods."

Jessica picked up the tickets from her plate and followed him into the kitchen. "Patrick Henley, these are for a Metal Thunder concert — tonight!"

"I know. That's why I'm hurrying. We're going to have a big night, you and I. It's the nine o'clock show at the Civic Center in St. Cloud." He dribbled soy sauce into the wok and watched the steam.

"Patrick, I haven't seen you for more than thirty seconds for a week and all of a sudden you're in my house, making me dinner and taking me to a rock concert?"

"I thought you could use some cheering up."

She poked him in the ribs with her fingers. "Okay, okay." He laughed. "I thought I could use some cheering up, too. Work in the real world can be tough. I miss you, Jessica. I miss being with you, so I tracked down your mother, set this up, and voilà. Tomorrow I'm taking you to the game where I'll shoot lots of pictures of you at your best. You might be so happy after all this, that you'll be proud of Daniel, too. He thought this was a great idea. He's a little worried about you."

"Daniel? I don't know . . . maybe . . ." Jessica replied. She looked back at the tickets. "Wow, Metal Thunder."

Patrick kissed her. "What's the point in making money if you can't spend it on someone you love?"

The next night the gym was packed, the bleachers overflowing with students, faculty and parents, familiar faces from around town, and men and women Tarenton hadn't seen in years. It seemed strange to the squad to see the other cheerleaders in red and white, even if their uniforms were thirty years out of date.

The opposing basketball team, busy dribbling and shooting in their white knee-length shorts, was good, even if their heads were dotted with bald spots and sprinkled with gray hair.

Nick Stewart arrived with Nancy Goldstein and Pres and Mary Ellen, and when the cheerleading squads gathered at the designated corner, he took a minute to congratulate Melissa again and introduce her to Nancy. When he and Pres had gone to their seats, the two squad captains went over their cheers and signals so each would have equal time on the floor.

"I hope you enjoy cheering as much as I did," Nancy said to Melissa.

"I'm looking forward to it," Melissa replied. "The squad went out on a limb for me. I hope I'm worth it."

As the group split up, Mary Ellen touched Olivia's arm. "Could I talk to all of you for a minute?" She waited until she had everybody's attention and then looked back at the captain. "I wanted you all to know, and I wanted you to hear from me, that I'm giving up my job at Garrison. I'll finish out the contract, but that's it. I love cheering, but I still love Tarenton and I decided not to coach until I find a position that won't conflict with my feelings."

She laughed at the sudden grins on everyone's faces. "I knew you'd think I made the right choice," she added before she trotted back to her squad.

The squad sat back on the bench as the teams finished dribbling. Jessica watched her stepfather as he jumped and put a perfect hook shot through the hoop. She could hardly believe it.

Melissa's attention was on the other end of the court, where Troy Fredericks slam-dunked the last ball for the high school. He turned around as he crossed the floor to his seat and winked at her. She waved and then laughed off Sean's and Peter's teasing. It felt so good to have them laughing with her that she could have hugged them both.

They were all quiet and in their seats, however,

as the drum roll began and the president of the PTA stepped forward with her microphone. "Ladies and gentlemen, Tarenton Wolves from all generations, welcome to the Alumni-Varsity Game. May I present the starting line-up for tonight's game."

Olivia brought the squad to its feet so they could cheer for each man as he ran into the center court and bowed. Pompons flying, she led them all, and when Daniel Bennett's name was called, the fans, many of whom remembered his skill, roared their approval. Pride hit Jessica like an unexpected slap on the back and as she jumped with her pompons, Patrick caught both of them in his lens, Jessica with her fabulous smile and her arms raised, Daniel watching her as if he remembered his own days in the gym. It would make a nice photograph.

When both basketball teams were introduced and the clowning had died down, the emcee continued with the cheerleaders. "For the Varsity team, may I present the cheerleaders from days gone by, the alumni squad captained by Mary Ellen Kirkwood Tilford." Pompons flying, Mary Ellen ran with the others onto the floor. Over the cheers, wolf whistles, and cat calls, her squad dipped into low curtsies. "Now," she whispered to Nancy and the two of them bounded into handsprings, exposing knee-length bloomers in red and white stripes.

The crowd rose to its feet and applauded. "And now for our varsity squad, cheering tonight for the alumni team."

Olivia hustled them out and waited for the

emcee to continue. "Tonight, the varsity squad is pleased to introduce its newest member, alternate Melissa Brezneski."

Melissa's heart thundered as she joined them. She turned and found Molly and her parents in the stands, holding up a hand-printed banner reading, WE LOVE MISSY. "So do we," Hope whispered from her spot next to her.

A blur of movement made Melissa turn. Diana Tucker was twisting from her seat and marching from the gym. Then Melissa felt the familiar pressure of Sean's hands on her waist. "This is it, Ballerina," he whispered as Olivia signaled for the cheer to begin.

Six voices repeated her name in unison as Sean supported her lift. The scissor kick was perfect. She threw her head back, her hair falling into place as she came down on her toes. Their cheer continued as the girls flanked her and all of them cartwheeled, putting Peter behind her for the final jump. Hands again gripped her waist . . . perfect balance, perfect timing. She bent her knees; he held her tightly and raised her jump an extra foot. Back again on her feet, Melissa knelt on one knee as the squad formed a semi-circle, all arms and pompons pointing at her. "M–E–L–I–S–S–A, she's the one to cheer today!"

The tension and nervousness were gone. Melissa beamed, jumped to her feet, and hurried back to the bench with the rest of them. The game began as she was hugged and slapped on the back.

I belong here, she thought. These guys are the best! She looked from one happy face to the other

. . . Sean, Olivia, Hope, Tara, Jessica, and Peter. Melissa was surrounded by the best friends she'd ever had. She was part of the team. She was where she wanted to be.

Sometimes the right guy is the one who has been there all along — even if he does belong to someone else! Read Cheerleaders #36, CHANGING LOVES.

It's a Night to Remember...

Last Dance

Sequel to Saturday Night!

by Caroline B. Cooney

Happiness and heartbreak are in the air. Eight months have passed since that special, memorable Autumn Leaves Dance. Now it's June, time for the last dance of the school year. Anne, wiser and more beautiful than ever, just wants to survive it. Beth Rose is more in love than ever...but wants Gary to fall in love with her, too. Emily, her safe world suddenly shattered, turns to Matt to make it right. Molly has been rejected, and she's out for revenge. Kip has been having the time of her life, and hopes the dance will be the perfect ending to the school year.

It will be romantic for some, heartbreaking for others...but above all, a dance the girls will never forget!

Look for it wherever you buy books!

$2.50 U.S./$3.95 CAN

Scholastic Books

LD871